SIX
MORE
MONTHS
OF JUNE

SIX
MORE
MONTHS
OF JUNE

Daisy GARRISON

FLATIRON
BOOKS
NEW YORK

SIX MORE MONTHS OF JUNE. Copyright © 2024 by Daisy Garrison. All rights reserved. Printed in the United States of America. For information, address Flatiron Books, 120 Broadway, New York, NY 10271.

www.flatironbooks.com

Grateful acknowledgment is made to Hannah Lachow for permission to quote from the poem "Six More Months of June."

The Library of Congress Cataloging-in-Publication Data

Names: Garrison, Daisy, author.
Title: Six more months of June / Daisy Garrison.
Description: First edition. | New York : Flatiron Books, 2024. | Audience: Ages 12–18.
Identifiers: LCCN 2023056411 | ISBN 9781250348678 (trade paperback) | ISBN 9781250348654 (hardcover) | ISBN 9781250348661 (ebook)
Subjects: CYAC: Interpersonal relations—Fiction. | Friendship—Fiction. | High schools—Fiction. | Schools—Fiction. | LCGFT: Novels.
Classification: LCC PZ7.1.G37636 Si 2024 | DDC [Fic]—dc23
LC record available at https://lccn.loc.gov/2023056411

Our books may be purchased in bulk for promotional, educational, or business use. Please contact your local bookseller or the Macmillan Corporate and Premium Sales Department at 1-800-221-7945, extension 5442, or by email at MacmillanSpecialMarkets@macmillan.com.

First Edition: 2024

10 9 8 7 6 5 4 3 2 1

To the class of 2016, who became the class of 2020

Of all the delectable islands the Neverland is the snuggest and most compact, not large and sprawly, you know, with tedious distances between one adventure and the next, but nicely crammed.

—*PETER PAN*, J. M. BARRIE

i could use six more months
of this feeling

. . .

even that wouldn't be enough

—"SIX MORE MONTHS OF JUNE," HANNAH LACHOW

SIX
MORE
MONTHS
OF JUNE

Mina

"And . . . we're recording."

"All right. Caplan Lewis." I picture him. I try to think what he'd want me to say, and then I realize I've been quiet for too long. "Sorry. Can we start over?"

"No, that was cute. Just keep going."

"Okay, right. So, Caplan Lewis is, well, you know. It's silly to describe him, since everyone knows Caplan."

The girl in charge makes a spinning motion with her hands and nods toward the boy recording. I think she means for me to look at the camera, which is obviously not happening. I look to the left of it, at the boy's shoulder, then at my knees.

"That's actually the bottom line of who he is, right there. Caplan is known. He always has been." I laugh. "You'd be hard-pressed to find a single student or teacher or person in this school, on this planet, who doesn't know and love Caplan Lewis. He is everyone's favorite person."

Caplan

"Rolling?"

"Yes."

"Mina Stern is my best friend."

They wait for me to say more.

"Yeah, that's all. No small thing, though. She's my favorite person."

1
Caplan

Sometime in March, the loudspeaker goes off in the middle of homeroom, calling Mina to the office, which is funny cause it's Mina.

"You're getting expelled," I say.

It gets a good laugh, but not from her. Mina can keep her face straighter than anyone I know, especially if people are looking at her. She'll tell me sometimes, after the fact, that she was trying not to laugh or cry or roll her eyes, and I'll think she's lying, because her face was so pale and still.

I remember just as she's out of the room about the day they called her to the office because of her dad, and then I feel like a dick.

She still isn't back when I'm on my way to the office myself to do the morning announcements and everything before first period. When I get there, she's standing in front of the principal's desk with her arms crossed, and the principal and the vice are looking up at her all tense. I'm worried for a second that something terrible did happen.

She turns and sees me. "Caplan should do it."

I step up next to her.

"It is tradition," the principal says, "for the—"

"But I can't do it, and Caplan will be happy to."

"Sure I will," I say. "Do what?"

He starts again. "It is tradition for the valedictorian to speak at graduation."

I turn to Mina, but she won't look at me. She goes into some point then that I don't really follow, about democracy and the voice of the people.

The principal sighs. "Are you suggesting we hold a vote for the graduation speaker?"

"I'm suggesting we already have. Caplan is class president. He should give the speech."

I ran for class president on a dare from Quinn. This is sort of common knowledge, I think. My only real duties are the morning announcements and leading pep rallies.

"The speech is supposed to be an honor, and it is ideally"—he looks at both of us, Mina in her sweater vest, arms folded over her books, and me in my TDHS soccer windbreaker, probably with a pretty vacant expression. I realize I'm chewing gum and swallow it quickly—"of a certain tone."

Mina waits for me while I do the announcements. Walking back to class, she says, "You did a little fist pump. When you announced the Chess Club's tournament win."

"So?"

"So, no one can see you. They can only hear you." She's got a small smile in her voice. "I didn't know you were such fan of chess."

I give her a shove. "I didn't realize I was doing it," I say.

She's still smiling to herself.

"Stop paying attention to me," I say.

"Okay," she says, and she turns the corner to go to AP calc, which I am not in, without saying bye.

"I don't want to make a speech at graduation, either," I call to her.

"Heavy is the head that wears the crown," she calls back.

We bitched back and forth for weeks about the grad speech. I told her I'd deliver it if she wrote it, and she told me she had nothing to say about our high school or anyone in it. I told her that was a pretty mean and lofty thing to say, and she narrowed her eyes and asked me how many people I could say something nice about. I sat down and started to try to write one good thing about each person in our grade. I got tired after about fifty kids. I thought that was pretty impressive, but she just laughed at me. You cannot stand up at graduation, she said, and say that Jamie Garrity once held the side door open for you when you were running late. I told her I could write a really nice speech about her, or Quinn, or Hollis even, and that the whole idea of a graduation speech was dumb, and everyone should just each get to say one good thing about one person they really know and call it a day. She liked that. Like foot-in-the-door feelings, she said. When I didn't get it, she went on, "Like, the door is closing, it's your last chance, what do you still need to say?" Anyway, that's how we came up with the idea. I think the principal was so tired of talking about it that he said yes.

The day I film my part of the video is the first day of June—shorts-and-sweatshirt weather, really blue sky. After I film it, I head back to the cafeteria and cut through to the outdoor tables. Everyone's at the usual spot, and then there's Mina off on a bench with her book.

"CAP-O!" Quinn calls out, and I raise my hand to him as I pass by on my way to Mina's bench.

"You're outside," I say.

"It's a nice day," she says, not looking up from her book.

"Come on." I take the book, which I know will really annoy her. Once when we were little, I threw her book into the sand at the lake, and she didn't talk to me for days.

"Give it back."

"You know I will. I don't know how to read."

"Ha ha."

"Come eat with us."

She crosses her arms, then crosses her legs.

"It won't kill you. It's lunchtime. It's a perfect day. It lured you from the library. Come socialize." I take a step back, toward my friends, with her book.

"CAP!" Quinn yells again. "Stop flirting."

This makes Mina almost smile. Really, she just presses her lips together.

"How are you going to make friends next year at Yale if you don't start now?" I ask.

For a second, she looks like she's going to start yelling.

Then she just says, "It's a little late for me, with all of them, don't you think?"

"Mina, is he bothering you? Want me to beat him up?" Quinn yells.

She laughs then and leans around my shoulder, probably checking for Hollis, who I'm pretty certain is sitting up on top of the table, holding court. I don't know for sure. We were on a break right then, so I was in the habit of trying to never look at her directly, just at the edge of things, off to the side. This is sort of easy to do because of her hair, which is really long and reddish blond and always swinging around.

Mina sees her, or something else ominous, cause she shakes her head.

I hold out her book. When she reaches for it, I grab the strap of her bag and turn toward the others, so she has to walk along backward behind me.

2

Mina

Caplan drags me places. When we were little, he'd physically pull me—out into the water at the dunes, into the
snow when school was canceled, horror movies before
we were seventeen, the middle of the gym at dances—
and then eventually, he did it just by existing. Since
Caplan went ahead and became the most insufferably
physically ideal and athletically competent person on
the planet, that meant I went to soccer games. I always
sat with his mom and his little brother in the stands
above the students' section, with them all between us,
this bright roaring sea—girls with his number on their
cheek and boys chanting, *O Caplan! my Captain!* Drunk
and happy and part of it all. I wasn't part of it, but I
was there watching it, and that's something. He was like
a magnet. Or the sun. It would have been more embarrassing if I were the only one, but everyone sort of
orbited around him. The sun is bright and warm, and
all that.

Sometimes I felt grateful, and others I didn't. The first true warm day of senior spring, right around the time when we were all filming those godforsaken videos, he got me to eat lunch with his friends by taking my book. I knew he was doing it because Hollis was watching, and they were on one of their breaks. I didn't like it when he used me like that. First of all, it never works because there is no universe in which I would be a romantic threat. It is a transparent joke, just like me sitting at a lunch table with people like Quinn Amick and Hollis Cunningham.

I tug my book back for something to do with my hands when we get there. No one's really eating anymore. Hollis is sucking on the last of a Popsicle, and it's turned her mouth red. I make a bet with myself that they'll be back together by the end of the week. She has Quinn's baseball cap on, the one he always wears with the tiny stitched tree. Ah, love and war. Caplan sits down and pulls one of the other boy's half-eaten sandwiches toward him.

"Where were you?" someone asks.

"Filming my video," he says, mouth full.

"I can't believe Mina nabbed him," says Quinn. "Who am I gonna get to say something nice about me now?"

I look at Caplan just as he looks at Hollis. She's meeting his eyes with a blank expression, resting the Popsicle against her mouth. I should probably clarify: Hollis is the scariest person who has ever lived.

"I'll do it for you," she says, turning to Quinn.

"Aw, really, Holly?"

She bites off the last of the Popsicle and flicks the naked stick at him as one of her friends looks forlornly at her. Probably Hollis had already agreed to do her video.

"Why not? It doesn't matter." She looks at Caplan for a second, and then at me.

It's always an unpleasant surprise when I spend so much time observing, peaceful and invisible, and then suddenly someone decides to look at me. It's why actors never look directly into the camera, unless they're being uncanny on purpose.

"Mina," Hollis says, like she's just noticed me standing there, "Friday's my birthday."

"Oh," I say. "Happy birthday."

"No," she laughs. "You're so funny. I mean I'm having a birthday party. My mom's making me, just a thing at my house. Will you come?"

I stare at her. "Um. Yes, sure."

"Well, don't do me any favors," she says.

"No, yes, I'd love to. Thank you."

The bell rings, and Caplan stoops to pick the Popsicle stick up off the ground. He marches toward the trash cans with it, and Hollis sighs, stands, and follows him.

"They're getting boring, aren't they?" Quinn says to no one in particular as I let myself be carried back inside on their tide. Everyone vaguely agrees, and everyone still sort of watches them, standing by the bins, both looking very bright in the sun, the wind lifting their hair, red and gold, beautiful.

.   .   .

As we all condense, trying to shove through the cafeteria doors, I brush up next to one of Hollis's friends—Becca, the one who wanted Hollis to do her grad video. She gives me an unusually overtly bitchy look, so I speed up. In the hallway, I bend down to retie my laces, and she bumps into me from behind. As she passes, she says, "Down, dog," for her friends. I've fallen forward onto my hands and knees, so I take a second to make sure my face is empty, then I stand up and keep walking to physics.

For a while in middle school, they'd say, "Woof woof," every time they passed me. I assumed it generally meant loser or ugly, but I didn't know for sure so I tried not to care. I just started wearing headphones. This aligned pretty well with my then-recent commitment to not look at or speak to anyone unless absolutely necessary. They'd tortured me for years for always having my hand in the air, for being a show-off and a know-it-all, and then when I tried to go silent and invisible, they only hated me more. The hypocrisy would have been funny if I'd been in any state to laugh.

The first time I heard the *woof, woof* punch line was in eighth grade, a few months into my silence, in the girls' bathroom. "Mina Stern follows Caplan Lewis around like a puppy."

After the girls left, I came out of my stall at the same time as Lorraine Daniels. We used to have playdates as little kids, because our moms were friendly and she lived nearby. Then my dad died, and my mom got weird, and probably so did I. Plus, Lorraine moved. We still sat next to each other in classes sometimes, though. She wore thick red-framed glasses and got plenty of shit for it, but she never changed them or got contacts. I envied her conviction. She was quiet and smart, and I used to wonder if maybe we could be real friends, but she seemed to genuinely prefer being left alone. I guess I probably come off that way, too.

"They're jealous," she said, washing her hands, not looking at me, which I appreciated, because I was crying.

"What? They are. Strawberry Shortcake likes him. She was saying so before you came in."

This dig didn't really work because Hollis is like five nine.

"And honestly, he follows *you* around."

I know time is supposed to heal all things, but that memory has actually sharpened with age, grown edges, because it's the first time I can remember realizing the truth. Spending most of my time with Caplan didn't make me brighter or better. It made me duller, by contrast. And beyond that, I was not the only one who thought it was a miracle that he wanted to be my friend.

The fact that we had sailed together pretty blissfully through all of childhood attached at the hip is entirely to his credit. He never, not even in the pits of middle school, stopped wanting to do elaborate handshakes with me in the hallway or tried to make me his secret friend. There was never that adolescent moment when he realized it would be easier for him, that his world would make more sense, if he left me behind or at least excluded me from some parts of his life. That just never happened. Caplan does whatever he wants and very rarely wonders what people will think. The spring of our sophomore year, he tore something and couldn't run track. Out of boredom and curiosity and, let's be honest, a true proclivity for being the center of attention, he auditioned for the play, which was *Romeo and Juliet*. And of course he was good at it, of course he lit the whole thing on fire and made it indisputably cool.

At his audition, he flattened the crumpled printout of his speech on the floor at his feet in case he forgot the lines. The director noticed the rudimentary scanning, a simplified key I made up to help guide him through the rhythm. They asked Caplan where he learned about iambic pentameter, and Caplan said he had no clue what that was, but a friend had helped him practice. After he got the part, they asked me if I wanted to participate in the play, too, as a dramaturge. I had to look up what that meant. In the end, I said no, because it sounded like too much talking to other people, but I agreed to type up some packets about scansion and fair Verona, Italy, to be passed out on the first day of rehearsal.

Caplan and I spent hours that spring learning lines. The standing onstage and looking like a movie star part came pretty naturally to him, but for the words, their meaning, and the memorization, he needed me. That is perhaps Caplan's only arena of doubt—that he's not smart—maybe because it took him a little longer to learn to read, a million years ago. I remember watching him work, intense and stubborn, to understand it all and to say it all correctly, and I was floored.

How, I thought, is it possible that you are this person, all one thousand versions of you? How is it that you are going to be the varsity soccer captain, the prom king,

president of some fraternity someday, and also be this
boy on my bedroom floor memorizing Shakespeare, face
pressed into my carpet, asking me what consequences
yet hang in our stars?

3
Caplan

I knew Hollis was going to follow me to the trash cans. That's a good thing about being stuck on the dance floor with someone. You know their moves.

When I turn around, she's just standing there looking at me. I wait for her to talk, but she won't. Hollis does conversation like she's playing chicken.

"You shouldn't litter," I say.

"You had to do the video with Mina?"

"Why do you care?" I say.

"Like together? In a pair? Like fucking wedding vows?"

"You broke up with me."

"Oh, you noticed?"

"Hollis." I pinch the bridge of my nose.

"What? What do you want, Caplan?"

"I want you to take Quinn's fucking hat off," I say to my hand.

She pulls it away from my face, takes the hat off, and tosses it to me. She's sort of glaring and sort of smiling.

"You didn't have to do that to Mina. In front of every-one."

She stops smiling.

"If you wanted me to come to your birthday party, you could have just asked me," I say.

"Maybe it isn't about you. Maybe sometimes I'm just nice."

I snort.

"Would you have come to my birthday if I'd just asked you?"

"Well, yeah. We'll always be like. Friends, yeah."

I'm messing with Quinn's hat in my hands. I make myself look at her. She looks like she's about to cry but doesn't seem embarrassed at all. For a second, neither of us says anything. The bell rings.

"And I didn't break up with you. I said we should take some space. To think," she says.

"Well," I say. "Have you? You know. Thought?"

She laughs. "I wasn't the one who needed to think."

"So you did it to see what I'd do."

"Yeah."

"Just to get a reaction out of me."

"Mm-hm."

"Well. That was sorta childish, don't you think?"

"Oh my god." She throws her hands up. "Caplan, of course I did. What, have you never liked someone who is totally neutral about you?"

She waits for me to respond. I really hate that. When I can feel her leading us somewhere, setting me up to say something specific.

"Okay, fine, congratulations, you are the biggest grown-up of all, the least jealous, the least emotional. Good for you." She starts to walk away.

The freshmen trickle out into the lunch yard in little clusters, glancing over at us.

"Can we go somewhere else to talk?" I ask, rocking back and forth on my heels. "Did you drive today?"

"I am not skipping class to go sit in my car and listen to you call me a child."

"I didn't call you a child. I said you did something childish."

She stares at me. She shakes her head and starts to turn.

"And I'm not," I say, really much louder than I'd have liked to, "I'm not neutral. About you."

"Thank you. Thank you so much. That's beautiful."

A full table of freshmen stare at us openly.

"Really, you should write that down. You should write a whole book. You should—"

"What class do you have right now?" I ask.

"Study hall."

"Hollis, Jesus, can you just—? I want to talk, I came over here to talk to you. Can we just—"

"Just what? Have the same fight again? Why?"

"Because fighting with you is fun and interesting."

"Okay." She makes a face like, *And?*

"And I miss it."

She glares at me for another second, a classic Hollis look, furious, blazing, so fucking pretty.

"And I'd rather fight than not talk to you."

She blazes at me some more. Then, she sighs and walks right past me. She's almost at the parking lot before she turns back. "Well. Are you coming?"

Here is the story of how Mina and I became friends. It starts with her being a child genius, and my being an evil little prick. We met in second grade. It was one year after my dad left us and we moved from Indiana to Two Docks, Michigan, into a small, square, white house on Corey Street, directly across from a redbrick castle with a blue front door and a big brass knocker. For me, given the way I was turning out, this was just in time.

No one ever taught Mina to read. She was a PTA legend. One day, when she was like three years old, and I was probably still learning to talk, she was in the car with her mom and her dad. They were arguing about something and they missed their turn. She called out from her car seat that Alpine Street was back that way. When they asked her how she knew, she said she saw the sign. They spent the rest of the afternoon driving around pointing at street signs in our town, and she just rattled them off—Willow, Gates, Brighton—silent *gh* like it was nothing—Huron, Muncie, Beaufort, fucking Beaufort.

I remember wanting to smash my nuggets into the face of the lady telling the story the first time I heard it. Why was she taunting my mom with lore of this freak genius who lived right across the street from us, this Mozart of chapter books, when her own son was seven and a half years old and could not, for the life of him, get his *b*'s and *d*'s straight? After that night, my mom constantly suggested playdates or plans to get our families together. I was sure she thought hanging out with Mina would rub off on me and make me smarter. Looking back, I think maybe she was just lonely without my dad and looking to make friends, even before she knew Mina's mom would soon be raising a kid on her own, too. I don't know.

Meanwhile, we had entered into the hellscape of reading out loud in class. I was already good at soccer and kind of ran shit on the playground, so it was probably awesome for the other kids to see me down bad and eating my own humiliation every day when we'd go around the room in a snaking train for doom with the teacher pointing at each one of us in turn. I always got through like four words. Then everyone would laugh, and the teacher would move on. That fall, we had assigned seats next to each other. After my caveman stutter, in a cruel and obvious twist of fate, it would be Mina's turn. She had a really nice, clear voice, didn't speed up to show off on purpose, and didn't monotone or forget when to breathe. She sounded wise and peaceful, but also like there was a secret she wasn't saying, something else just behind the words that she knew all about and would maybe tell us someday. She wasn't particularly popular, but everyone liked to listen to Mina read.

Anyway, I hated her guts. It felt to me, at eight, obsessed with myself and my own take on the world, that she was doing it on purpose and that she existed to make me look bad, in quiet opposition to the natural rules and order of the world in which I thrived. She would literally read during recess. This point especially infuriated me. Recess was for yelling and running and kicking balls. Stuff I was awesome at. And so, I internalized all my tiny rage, and I bullied her. I was a coward, and bad with conflict even then, so none of it happened to her face. But to anyone who would listen, I called her a nerd, and a freak, and a loser. Obviously not super creative, but it was surprisingly easy to bring everyone on board. I called her *four-eyes* and *bug-eyes*. I said her freckles were a contagious geek disease. I said her hair was so long and dark because she was a witch. I waged my war on her entirely underground, and overnight, other kids were re-peating it all to her face. Mina was different and special. I pointed this out, and we all turned away from her.

She bore it all like a fucking boss, which only made me more mad. She never reacted, or cried, or told anyone. It was like she couldn't hear us at all, or if she could, she didn't care. That's how far above us she was. Then, on Hal-loween, when we all came to class in costume, she wore giant fake glasses that magnified her eyes and colored in all her freckles with green and black, and of course, she wore a witch's hat. It is difficult to explain, at the time, how baller this was of her.

A week later, Ms. Levi decided to rub it in my face, which probably altered the course of my life. She held Mina and me after class before lunch one day and ex-plained that from now on, we would be in our own reading group, just us two. Mina and I were going to be reading partners. Even though I was the class dunce, I was smart enough to know that this was be-cause Mina was brilliant and I was stupid and I needed her help. I stormed from the room, and Mina came running after me.

"Wait! Where are you going?"

"To recess, to be with my friends. Leave me alone."

"Just hold on a minute." She was panting, jogging to keep up with me. "What is making you sadmean?"

"Sadmean?"

"You're sad, so you're being mean."

"That isn't a real word. Why are you so weird?" But she had confused me enough to get me to stop walking. I wanted to understand. I didn't want to feel stupid. "Is it different from just plain-old *mean* mean?"

"Yes. I wouldn't talk to you if you were being *mean* mean. I don't have time."

I looked at her, and I felt guilty. It was a brand-new and deeply uncomfortable feeling.

"I'm sorry I called you weird."

"It's okay. Everyone does."

"I'm sorry for that, too."

"Well, that's silly. It's not your fault."

I was quiet.

"People called me weird way before you moved here."

This should have relieved me, but I just felt worse. "I'm sorry about your dad, too."

"Oh," she said. "Thank you."

I shuffled my feet. She wouldn't stop looking at me. It made me nervous.

"I met him once," I said. "He gave me a shot."

"Well, that was his job," she said.

"Yeah, but it didn't really hurt."

She eyed me skeptically. "Shots always hurt."

"Well, this one was not so bad. Cause of how your dad did it."

"How he did it?"

"I just wasn't scared," I said, annoyed now that I'd said anything.

"Well. I always thought he was a good doctor. But it's nice to know from someone else."

"Sure."

"So. Why are you sad?"

I sighed. "Because reading is impossible. I'd rather get ten shots than read one page."

"Do you really mean that?"

"Almost, I think," I said.

"Well, you're wrong. And you'll see." And with that, she was off down the hallway, and then I was following her.

We had this homework where we were supposed to read for thirty minutes every single night. That afternoon, Mina crossed the street and knocked on my front door, and my mom let her in. She marched into my bedroom, completely at home, with the first *Harry Potter* under her arm.

"You gotta be kidding," I said. "That's like a billion pages long."

"It's a good story, so you'll be happy that it lasts."

And for the next thirty minutes, timed out exactly on my new waterproof digital watch, we read out loud to each other. Mina would read five pages, and I would read two—stumbling, slowly, but reading all the same. She was right, it was a good story, and the thirty minutes went quick. That night, after dinner, I was wandering around the house, wondering what would happen next to the boy who lived in the cupboard under the stairs.

"I'm going for a walk," I announced. My mother appeared out of nowhere, blocking the front door with her arm. She was in her scrubs, fresh off a long shift at work.

"It is almost eight o'clock, Caplan. You're going nowhere."

I sighed. "I'm going to see Mina Stern. Across the street. I need more reading help."

These were magic words. My mother smiled this annoying grown-up smile and let me pass. I crossed the street in the dark, a little breathless with the lateness and strangeness of my successful escape. I stood for a moment at her front door, feeling awkward. I wandered around the side of the house till I saw a high window, slightly open. White curtains with little silver stars were floating out in the breeze. The roof that jutted out over the side porch just under the window was only a foot or so from the top of her jungle gym, so I climbed up and called out toward the stars. The curtain was tugged aside, and there she was, in a purple nightgown covered in planets and rocket ships. I took exactly one second to be startled by the blue of her eyes without glasses, and then she slid the window open farther and asked me what in the world I was doing, and was I looking to fall and break my neck?

"I'm here to read," I had said. "I gotta know what happens next."

And you'll find that there are certain things you cannot go through without becoming friends. Fighting a fully grown mountain troll is one. Reading the entire *Harry Potter* series out loud together past bedtime is another.

"What are you thinking about?" Hollis asks me. We're lying in the back of her car with the seats down and a blanket up against the trunk's window.

"Mm, nothing," I say, not opening my eyes.

"It's fascinating," she says, "that boys can actually think about nothing."

"What do you mean?"

"Like I've realized you have whole periods of time where you are literally, like, not having a thought. You're just zoned out. White noise."

"And you don't ever have that?"

She laughs, her head bouncing up and down on my stomach. "No, I'm kind of always having a thought."

"That sounds exhausting."

"Mm-hm."

"You need a nap, I bet," I say, pulling her up closer to me. "What are you thinking about now, then?"

"I'm thinking," she says, tucking her chin on top of my shoulder, "that it's actually inherently childish to *call* your girlfriend childish. It's sexist."

"So are you my girlfriend again?"

She smiles into my shoulder. I pull her onto me so that she's lying flat on her stomach. She lines up her arms and legs with mine and our faces press together, cheek to cheek, so I'm looking one way and she's looking the other. She pushes her palms down flat into mine. This is our tradition, our joke about cuddling when you're in a car, maximizing surface area and space, touching as much of each other as possible. "I want no part of my body to touch the literal back seat of my family's car," she'd said the very first time we did it. To be fair, Hollis drives a massive white Suburban. Quinn once told her that if that was the car her parents were going to buy, they were expecting her to have sex in it. She threw something at him and said it was so she could pick up all her younger siblings from school. I can remember that day so clearly, early fall our junior year, Hollis swinging her car keys around on a long TDHS lanyard, freshly licensed. We'd lost our virginities pretty recently to each other. The whole conversation at the lunch table, the acknowledgment that we were having sex, made me turn bright red. Everyone was giving me shit, but Hollis didn't seem embarrassed. She looked actually very pleased with herself. Proud. I remember that it made me feel so good. So cool.

"You're all sweaty," she says.

"Well, so are you."

"No, that's your sweat, not mine. I'm covered in your sweat."

"Gross."

We lie there happily for a bit.

"I can't believe you're thinking about the 'childish' thing right now."

"I'm not anymore. It was a passing thought. It was passing through before, right when you asked me," she says.

I consider it.

"Well. You're right, I think," I say, "but say some more about it. For my white-noise boy brain to understand."

"I'm not saying I was behaving super well. I was just thinking your word choice—"

"My word choice. Jeez—"

"*Childish.* It puts you so far above me."

"Well. I don't think I'm above you. At all."

"Good," she says. "You're not."

"This time, actually, I was under you. That was a fun switch-up."

She smacks her hand down onto mine.

"To be clear," she says, "I *was* being childish. And I knew it. And you knew it. And I want you to be truthful. And to call me on my shit. I just want you to feel sexist while you do it."

I burst out laughing. It makes both our bodies shake, which makes her laugh, too.

"No more stunts to figure out how I feel, then," I say.

"Maybe if you ever just told me how you feel, I wouldn't need to go there." She scoots down so she's propped her elbows on my chest with her chin on her hands.

"Caplan."

"Yes."

"Will you come to my birthday?"

"Yes, Hollis. I will."

"Is our fight over?"

"You tell me."

She kisses me. Somewhere in the car, my phone starts vibrating.

"We should probably go to class," she says, rolling off me.

"Oh, whatever, second-semester seniors," I say, fishing my phone from the front seat. There's a missed call from my mom. She's also texted me about a hundred times.

> You have an email from your Michigan Portal!

Then,

> CALL ME!

Then,

> I LOVE U no matter what.

"Oh, fuck," I say.

"What?" Hollis says.

"No, nothing." I scramble to pull my boxers on,

socks, shoes, shirt, then tug my shoes off again to put on my pants. I almost kick Hollis in the face.

"Cap, hey, what's wrong?"

"Nothing, nothing," I say. "I just forgot about something I have to deal with. I gotta go, I'm sorry. I'll text you."

"Wait, I have to go, too. Just give me a sec," she says, messing with her bra.

"You're telling me you don't want to take your time, brush your hair fifty times, and use your face misty thing and stuff?"

She narrows her eyes. "Fine, go."

I'm halfway out of the car already, but I kiss her again. Then I book it for the school side door, praying someone will be hanging around to let me in.

4

Mina

I'm standing up at the board in physics, taking my turn to complete an equation, when I notice Caplan in the hallway, through the clear window of the classroom door. His face is all flushed, and he's hopping around like he needs to pee. He beckons at me to come. I turn back to the board. After a minute, I look back, and he's making a *please* prayer with his hands.

"Mina?" Ms. Turner asks, "all set?"

"Sorry, almost."

The classroom door opens, and Caplan sticks his head in. "Hi, Ms. T. Sorry to bother you—"

She looks up from the quizzes she's grading. "Caplan, what can I do for you?"

I have no idea how the AP Physics teacher knows Caplan's name or when they would have met.

Caplan gives her a dazzling sheepish smile. "They need Mina in the office for a minute."

"Oh," she says, going back to her quizzes. "All right, just let her finish."

I shake my head at Caplan, and he smirks. I finish the equation and turn to stand next to it, hands folded.

Ms. Turner looks up. "That's correct. You may go," she says, and then she calls on the next student.

As she looks away again, Caplan swings my bag off my chair and takes it with us.

"So I'm not coming back?" I ask him once we're in the hallway.

"It depends what it says."

"What *what* says?"

His showman energy's all gone. He looks like he's going to throw up.

"Caplan, what's going on?"

He just shakes his head and tries to drag me with him into the boys' bathroom.

I brace myself against the doorframe. "Nope."

"Come on, it's empty."

"Absolutely not."

"Mina, please—"

"Tell me what's going on."

He shoves his phone into my face, still trying to pull me into the bathroom. There's a notification—an email from the University of Michigan. He's been on the wait list for almost two months. I stop gripping the doorframe, and we both stumble into the bathroom. Caplan throws himself into a stall and sits down on the ground with his back against the door.

"Are you throwing up?" I ask.

"Can you just open it?"

"I can't open it. You need to do that."

"Mina. Please. Open it."

"Look, it's gonna be okay—"

"I will do anything for you to just open the fucking email."

"Okay, okay," I say.

His password is his mom's birthday, 0223.

"It says there's been an update on your portal."

He groans and bangs the back of his head into the door.

"You want me to check it?"

"Yeah."

"What's your log-in?"

"My school email," he says, "and password Malfoy-boy17. Capital *M*."

I swallow my laugh, hold it for later. "Hey, Caplan."

"Yeah."

"You're my best friend."

"You're my best friend, too, Meen. Are you saying that because I didn't get in?"

"No, give me a second."

I reload the page. The whole truth of the moment swoops down on me and knocks all my organs around as the wheel at the top of the page spins. I have half a breath to hope, to pray, which I've never really done, that he will get in, that he will win, that he will always get in and win for the rest of his life. Then Hollis texts him—

You left the condom in my car

It was stuck to Kelly's lacrosse stick

We're going to jail for that

The Michigan page updates.

"Caplan, come out here."

"Are you crying?"

"Come here."

"Fuck," he says, "motherfuck shit goddamn." He bangs the door open, one arm crooked over his face, and holds out his hand for his phone. He looks at it for a second. Then he looks up at me, struck dumb.

I'm smiling so hard it hurts, and I'm definitely also crying.

"I got in?"

"You got in."

He whoops. He howls at the ceiling and throws his fists into the air like he does when someone on their team scores in soccer, and then he's crushing me to him, picking me up, swinging me around.

"Put me down," I say, laughing, "and call your mom."

"My mom!" he shouts. "Oh my god, I gotta call my mom."

He picks up my bag and turns to leave and then presses it into my hands.

"Sorry, this is yours, sorry, what the fuck?" He's running his hands through his hair and shaking his head and smiling like the sun. "I can't believe this," he says.

"Well, I can."

"Mina . . . it's *Michigan*."

"Yeah. But it's also you, Caplan."

He hugs me one more time, fast and tight, and then he's gone, practically skipping.

I stand in the hallway for a bit with my arms wrapped around myself. I wonder how it would feel to know so completely what you wanted to do and where you were supposed to be. Of course Caplan knows. He thinks of himself as a simple person, he's said so before, but really he's just pure. There is nothing dark in Caplan. Nothing twisted or buried away. I shake myself. Sometimes being around him for short periods of time makes me feel like this after, almost how I'd imagine a hangover would feel. Like I'm in withdrawal. I run blue. It's a real letdown sometimes to return to myself, once he's gone from me. If I run blue, then Caplan runs gold.

I lean against the wall for a bit longer, being dramatic. Then I take my time wandering back to physics.

5
Caplan

Late that afternoon, I'm double-parked to pick Mina up from work at Dusty's Books, so I'm leaning on the horn, but really I just feel like making noise. She comes out looking very classically Mina, annoyed, and trying not to laugh. She's also holding a big box.

"You're going to get me fired," she says, sliding into the seat and placing the box on my lap. It says BOOKS FOR MINA in black marker letters. I drive off so fast the tires screech.

"Cap, Jesus."

"You won't get fired," I say. "Sarah loves me."

"Yes, all women of a certain age love you."

"Hey. All women of any age love me."

She rolls her eyes and then puts the window down.

"Sorry," I say, "that was a joke."

"Shut up," she says.

"So, what's in the box?" I ask. "More books no one else wants?"

"No. I labeled it like that so I could hide it at work. It's a present for you."

I pull over and almost jump the curb.

"And get out," she says. "You're unbalanced. I'm driving."

As she stalks around the front of the car, I open the box. Inside is another box, a shoebox, and inside that is a pair of navy high-top Converse with yellow stitching and a yellow tongue. She pulls open the driver's-side door.

"Meen . . ." I say, picking up one shoe and turning it over in my hands. In more yellow stitching on the heel, it says CAP. She's leaning on the door, watching me.

"You didn't."

"Told you I was sure you'd get in."

"A departure from tradition?" I give her a nudge with the tattered black-and-white high-tops I have on.

"We're making new traditions," she says. "I figure you'll look fantastically douchey in them at tailgates and take many horrible Instagrams."

I get out of the car and hug her, with the one shoe still in my hand. "Thank you."

"It's nothing."

"It's not nothing. You really thought I'd get in."

She twists out of the hug. "I don't think things. I know them." She gets behind the wheel.

"I love when you act bitchy," I say fondly, climbing into the passenger's seat and immediately unlacing my black Converse to put on my new clown shoes. I look over and realize she's fully smiling.

"Get your feet off the dash."

"It's my dash. Why are you smiling like that?"

"Oh, nothing."

"No neverminds."

This was a thing we've said since we were little. With both our families down a man at eight years old, we often started thoughts we didn't want to finish out loud. But it did us both good to get them out, so we started saying *no neverminds*. Mina's idea. Child genius.

"You just really did listen to me, after all. About the acting-versus-being thing."

"The what thing?"

"I told you once that you were never allowed to call me or anyone else a bitch, but you could say I was acting like one. Or acting bitchy. Like, once a year. As long as I really was."

I think about Hollis, picking apart how I'd said she was being a child, acting childishly, whatever, and realize I haven't told Mina that we're back together.

"Wait, wrong way," I say.

"This is the way to your house."

"No, we're picking up Quinn, too. He's still at school. He had detention."

"What for?"

"Skateboarding in the hallway again, I think."

"Naturally."

As we're parked and waiting for Quinn to come out, Mina's smiling again. This is a lot of teeth in one day for Mina.

"What now?" I ask.

"I can't believe we could go to school together."

"Mina, come on."

"You come on," she says. "You don't think it would

be fun to come bother me in the library? How else do we know you'll ever see the inside of it?"

"Mina, you're going to Yale. You're committed."

"I could always back out," she says, like it's all a joke. "I got into Michigan, too, you know."

"Yeah, early, as, like, your backup."

"Michigan was not my backup. I'd be happy to go there. I'd have applied to more schools otherwise."

"Right, but you didn't, cause then you slam-dunked the dream. You got Yale," I say.

"Would you, like. Not want me at Michigan?" Her tone changes all at once. She looks at her hands on the steering wheel.

"No. What? Mina, I thought you were kidding."

Her knuckles are white.

"Hey, come on. Back to earth. Where'd you go?" I pull her hands off the steering wheel and put them in her lap.

"Sorry." She shakes herself. "I'm fine."

"No, stop it. Of course it would be awesome to go to school together. You're my best friend. That would be like—that would be so cool. I can't even think about it. I shouldn't think about it, and neither should you, because it's not happening. You belong at Yale."

"I feel like we belong together."

Something about the way she says it makes my face hot.

"Hey-O!" Quinn's voice comes floating in through the open window. He lopes down the school lawn, his skateboard thrust proudly overhead.

Mina gives me her profile, staring out the other window.

"What just happened?" I say to her shoulder.

"Never mind," she says, starting the car as Quinn gets in the back.

He's pulled the night air in with him. It puts my hair on end.

"I thought they said one more time and they were taking that away from you," Mina says, free and easy as anything, nodding at the skateboard as she pulls off down the dark street. I can't really see her face, though, because her hair is blowing around, hiding it.

"They can't touch me," Quinn says. Then he leans forward and bear-hugs me, practically climbing into the front with us. "LET'S FUCKING GO BLUE BABY!!!!!!!!!!!!"

"Put your seat belt on," says Mina.

"You're gonna let her talk to me like that in your car?"

"Yeah," I say, shoving him off me, "I am. Look what she got me." I stick my foot in his face.

"Holy shit," he laughs. "But you guys won't be matching anymore?"

"Bold," Mina says. "Bold of you to bring up my sneakers."

"Hey, come on," Quinn says, "everyone knows boys act like dicks in elementary cause they have a crush."

Mina rolls her eyes.

"But these are sick," Quinn says, inspecting the stitching.

"Jealous?" I ask.

"In your dreams, Captain."

Quinn was rejected from Michigan straight off the bat. He took it well. Quinn takes everything well.

"Red's more my color," he says. "Plus, the girls are hotter at Indiana. Oh, sorry, Mina."

He sits back and clicks in his seat belt.

"That's fine," she says, "don't pretend to be decent on my behalf."

"Oh, no, I'm deeply decent. Down to the bone. I meant I'm sorry because you got into Michigan, too, so obviously the best girls go there."

She sticks her tongue out at me. I don't think I have ever seen Mina stick her tongue out at anyone.

"Well, Mina's going to Yale," I say.

"I told you," she says, "I'm going wherever I want."

"Fuck yeah. Maybe Mina's rebelling," says Quinn. "Maybe she'll fuck the alma mater and finally live a little."

"Exactly," Mina says. "Quinn, you know what? For that, you can play your music."

"We should play my music," I mumble. "It's my car."

"It's your mom's car."

Quinn puts his on, and instead of telling him to quit yelling, Mina rolls all the windows down in the back, too, and sings along: "*Oh, baby, you, you got what I need*"—she turns to me, letting me back in, forgiving me—"*but you say he's just a friend.*"

Forgiving me for what? I don't even care. The air is cool and brimming with something, like it's the beginning of the year, not the end, and Mina's driving with one knee up, and Quinn's singing at the top of his lungs, arms outstretched and spanning the whole back seat, howling like a wolf at the moon. The streetlights race by, lighting up our little world and then dimming it again like an old movie, the shutter opening and closing: my two oldest friends, the day I got into school, driving me home.

6

Mina

For my eighth birthday, my dad bought me a pair of black high-top Converse, because I'd seen them on a billboard while we were in the car and said that they looked like something Harriet the Spy would wear, which was the book I was reading and rereading at the time. Someone on adventures, not worried about fashion, getting things done. Then, a month later, he died in a car accident on the same highway. He was less than a mile from the same billboard and the exit that would have brought him home to us. The other driver had a heart attack, so it wasn't anyone's fault. That was made very clear to me.

I wouldn't take the shoes off for anything, not the funeral, not for my first panic attack when my mother stripped me out of the rest of my clothes and stuck me in the shower to get me to calm down, and certainly not for school. When I walked into our third-grade classroom on the first day and Caplan Lewis, king of my torturers, was wearing the same shoes, I knew in my bones it could mean nothing good. Quinn Amick wasted no time in standing on his chair and pointing down, announcing to everyone that I was wearing boys' sneakers, because they matched Caplan's. Everyone laughed. At first, I continued to wear them just so they wouldn't know I cared, and then two weeks later, I did stop caring. Because my dad was gone. I continued to wear the shoes every day. People whispered that I probably didn't even take them off to sleep, and laughed, and then went back to their coloring and spelling.

Unfortunately, the word about my dad spread pretty quickly. He was one of three pediatricians in Two Docks. By third grade, almost all my classmates knew him in that background way you know certain adults in childhood. I think most of the parents used it as an opportunity to gently introduce their kids to the concept of death. It was different from a grandparent dying, and everyone could tell. It was a tragedy. I remember a lot of different adults using that word. I think they thought I wouldn't know what it meant, and my mom would. But my mom was sporadically catatonic at that point, still in the same white nightgown with blue flowers she'd been wearing for weeks, the one she put on the day she came home from work after getting the call, and I had an excellent vocabulary.

I'm not really sure if, from a psychological standpoint, we were helped or hurt by the fact he'd been such a known entity. At the time, I remember wishing everyone would stop staring at me, and the sad, awkward cloud of pity clung to me, making me an unideal candidate for playdates and birthday parties for the rest of my prepubescent experience. Then, of course, there were the birthdays I was invited to just because of my dad.

Ruby Callahan said it to my face, in her sweet earnest way: *I know we aren't friends, but my mom said I should include you cause, you know, and yeah.*

I did not attend. Every girl got a headband with a unique fake flower tacked on the side as a party favor, and they all wore them to school the next week.

I'm sure in some invisible way that I didn't appreciate back then, it was good to have the community mourning with me. I'm not claiming he was some kind of home-town hero. But, as the older lady who, after realizing my mother wasn't going to make eye contact with her at the funeral, leaned down to clasp both my hands in her cool leathered ones told me, "He was just a really wonderful guy." She smelled intensely of cinnamon gum, and she wore a sparkling elephant pin. That's all I remember from that day.

A few weeks after the funeral during free draw, when someone else, I think one of the girls, whispered loud enough for me to hear that I was actually wearing black sneakers because of my dead dad, I finally cracked and started to cry. Then something miraculous happened. Caplan Lewis slammed his fist down onto his desk, snapped the cap on his marker, and said very loudly, for all the class to hear, that maybe I wasn't wearing boy shoes. Maybe he was wearing girl shoes. I will never forget Quinn's face, mouth popped open in shock. No one made fun of my sneakers after that. Or my dad, for that matter. They made fun of plenty else, and Caplan remained recess royalty and acted like it hadn't happened, but from that day on, he wore the shoes every single day, too.

A few months later, we became reading partners and, eventually, friends, so I told him that my dad had given me the shoes for my last birthday. My next birthday that following summer, the first without him, was particularly bleak. My mom was still sleepwalking around and crying at strange times and definitely not up to cake, presents, or songs. But Caplan came home early from soccer day camp and surprised me. We watched the third *Harry Potter* movie, because we'd just finished the book. He brought cupcakes and grilled cheeses and a gift—a fresh pair of new black high-tops, exactly the same as my first pair but one size bigger, for me to grow into. When his birthday came around in March, I bought him a new pair, too. Converse don't hold up super well, especially if you wear them every single day. And that's what we've given each other for our birthdays, each year since. We don't wear them every day anymore. I'm well adjusted and normal and therapized within an inch of my life. But we still match sometimes—our four black high-tops slapping against hallway linoleum together, bearing on through it all.

Caplan's mom is working late at the clinic, so when we get to his house, she texts him to start on dinner. I call my mom and ask if she wants to join us, but it goes to voicemail. Then she texts me that she has a migraine again. My mom is objectively idle. She actually used to be quite an important librarian. She used to be a lot of things, I think, before my dad died, that now she is not.

I realize *important librarian* sounds like an oxymoron, but she was one of the very first people to successfully digitize the classification system in libraries, when the tides turned from all things analog. Then she consulted on the transition for what seemed like every library in the Midwest, from tiny church-basement operations to the big universities. I learned the Dewey decimal system before I learned my multiplication tables. And though my mother was a traditionalist at heart—she liked to collect what she called the "borrowing cards" from famous editions or favorite books, vanilla-colored slips with the list of readers who'd borrowed and loved them (sometimes multiple times in a row, or every five years, or just once, overdue, and then never again)—she was one of the people who figured out how to put the Dewey system into the computers and keep the books themselves on the shelves, when there were people who were considering libraries to be beyond use in totality, what with the internet and the growing popularity of e-readers. Things like the interlibrary loan, the literal act of sharing permanent and preserved physical knowledge, were possible because of her. I remember my father telling me she was like a superhero. That if it weren't for my mother and other librarians like her, all those books may have been packed up and left somewhere to gather dust or even, unthinkably, be thrown away. Books that had been handled and loved by so many being discarded was such a harrowing concept to me that I accepted it without question. My mother was indeed a super something. She'd saved the books, and the practice and community of a library, for everyone.

And for me, her daughter, she'd saved their borrowing cards. I memorized the decimal numbers at the top and made up lives and personalities for each person who'd borrowed the books. I imagined the discussions we would have, and the books I'd recommend to them, if they'd indeed loved *A Wrinkle in Time* (813.54, for North American fiction, 1945–1999) as much as I did. I think maybe she kept them for me because she felt guilty, doing away with the old system. Or maybe it wasn't guilt. Maybe she was just a recordkeeping enthusiast and couldn't quite let go of the past. This didn't serve her, of course, when my dad died.

Now I'm not even sure she reads. Eventually, she took off the white nightgown with blue flowers, but she never went back to work. I understood that it didn't really matter, since, after he died, the medical practice was sold, and I guess that money has kept us afloat this long. I'm not sure what we'll do if it runs out. My grandparents on my mom's side died before I was born, and my dad's family doesn't particularly like my mom and me. I think maybe we remind them of the fact that their son is gone, which is fair. Either way, I've never known people who are more passionate about being involved in the lives of people they don't seem to enjoy or approve of than my grandparents. They were super into the idea of me going to Yale, like my dad. They sent a very fancy flower arrangement when I got in. It was the first time I'd seen flowers in our kitchen since the funeral. My mom did not see how this was funny, but she did let me throw them out after I mentioned it.

When she asked me last August if I planned to apply, I was so surprised that I said yes. Of course. Because she was there with me, in the kitchen, in our life, participating. It was the closest we'd come in four years to saying my dad's name.

While we wait for Caplan's mom, we decide to make grilled cheese, because grilled cheese is Caplan's answer to anything—good times or bad—with Annie's Mac as our appetizer, and Oliver hears us banging around.

"Bro!" he yells from the top of the stairs. He comes down fast, two steps at a time and turned completely sideways, facing the banister and the kitchen and us. Oliver has always done stairs at this angle. I can picture him as a toddler, holding the same banister with both hands, putting one small foot and then another on each step. He's fourteen now.

"You're a dumbass," he says as he hugs Caplan, "but you're a dumbass who can do anything."

"Ollie, language, man," says Quinn.

"Actually, I'm going by Oliver, since I'm in high school now," says Oliver.

Quinn and Caplan bust up laughing.

"Dude!" Oliver says to Caplan.

"I think *Oliver* suits you," I say to Oliver.

"Thank you, Mina." He turns very red as he says it. He blushes worse than Caplan, since he's even fairer, with less eyebrows, more freckles. This makes Quinn and Caplan laugh even harder. Oliver has sort of always had a crush on me. He slams himself down into a chair.

"Whatever," he mumbles. "Congrats, dickhead."

I put the water on to boil, and the boys get out bread and cheese.

"All the freshmen are talking about how you and Hollis were fighting outside during our lunch and you made her cry," Oliver says. He turns to me. "They're so immature."

I try not to smile, head down in the pot.

"Hollis never cries," Caplan says, "unless she's trying to make a point. Oh yeah." He pulls Quinn's hat out of his backpack and shoves it into Quinn's chest. "She gave me this for you."

"So you're back on?" Quinn asks.

"Mm, yeah," Caplan says, returning to the bread, buttering carefully to its edges.

"Good work, soldier," Quinn says to his hat, and then he jams it back onto his head. "I guess post-college-acceptance energy helped?"

"Oh, actually, that was before. I left her car when I got the email."

"You did it in her car?"

Caplan laughs and shakes his head, trying to cover Oliver's ears with his hands, but Oliver swats him away.

The pot boils over suddenly.

"Sorry I didn't tell you," he says to me.

"I don't need to know about your vehicular sex," I say, hoping I sound funny.

"No, that we got back together."

"So you did. Get back together?"

"Yeah, I guess we did."

"Well, that's wonderful."

"Is it?"

"I don't have to go to her birthday anymore."

"Oh," he says, "right."

"And now I don't have to go to prom, either. It was looking dark there, for a second."

"I hate that joke," he says.

"What joke?" Quinn asks, eating shredded cheese straight from the bag.

The kitchen feels hot, with all the burners going. I take my sweater off.

"Stop that," I say, taking the cheese from Quinn.

"Wash your hands first or something. And it's not a joke. If Hollis and Caplan dump each other again before the prom, he's gonna drag me."

"You don't have a date to prom?" Oliver asks.

"What, you gonna take her to the ninth-grade dance?" Caplan says meanly, unlike himself.

"No, of course I don't," I say. "That's why Caplan knows he can count on me."

"You don't have a date," Caplan says, brandishing the tongs at me, "because everyone knows you don't want to go."

"I never said I didn't want to go," I say.

"Mina," Quinn says, getting down on one knee.

"Stop that," I say, pulling a handful of utensils from the drawer to set the table.

Quinn takes them from me and then gets back down on his knee. He holds up the knives and forks like they're flowers. "Mina Stern, will you please do me the honor—"

"Okay, fine," I say. "Fine, you're right, I don't want to go." I turn to Caplan. "Point made."

"Can you look at me and not at Cap for one fucking second," says Quinn. "I'm being serious."

"I was fucking around," Caplan says. "Mina would not be caught dead at prom—"

"Mina, if you actually wanted to, the ninth-grade dance needs chaperones—" says Oliver.

"EVERYONE SIT DOWN AND SHUT UP!" Quinn yells. "No, not you, Mina."

I stand. I cross my arms. "Quinn. Get up."

Quinn stays down, still holding out his silverware bouquet.

"Mina Stern," he says. "You are no one's benchwarmer,

and you are not too good to go to prom. Please get down off your very high horse—"

"Oh my god—"

"On which you look great, don't get me wrong, but get down off it, cause you're our friend and prom is the last big thing we're doing together and it'll be a good shit show and you have to be there. As my date. Cause someday you'll shake your Ivy League six-figure-job keys at me and I'll get to say I took you to prom way back when. Let me have that."

I turn to Caplan. He's recording us.

"Are you paying him to do this?" I ask.

"Nope," he says.

"Are you serious?" I say to Quinn.

"Hell yeah," he says.

"Okay. I'll go to prom with you if Caplan doesn't post that video anywhere."

Caplan and Oliver cheer, Oliver a little mournfully. Quinn drops all the utensils with a clatter and scoops me into a hug so tight my feet leave the floor.

It's a funny feeling. I can't think of the last time a boy who wasn't Caplan touched me. Then, all of a sudden, in the middle of all the joy, of course I do think of it. For one second, I'm worried I'll burst into tears, but Quinn stays hanging on to me so I have a moment to fix my face in his shoulder.

"You can't, like, wear a clown suit as a joke," I say as he sets me down.

"I swear," Quinn says, looking oddly flushed and bright-eyed, "it will be a totally serious, romantic, traditional prom."

"Never mind. Wear the clown suit."

"Okay. Maybe just the nose."

Then Julia, Caplan and Oliver's mom, comes in with yellow and blue balloons and cake with sparklers. There are tears and shouts and hugs all around. We've burned the sandwiches, so we start again, and we have a competition to see who can make the best grilled cheese, for Caplan to judge. I win, with cheddar and hot sauce on whole wheat. Eventually, there's a soft knock at the door, almost lost in all the happy noise. It's my mother, looking sleepy like a child, in her athleisure from yesterday, but smiling and holding a bottle of champagne. The Lewises don't have champagne glasses, so we pour it into Solo cups, and Caplan swigs straight from the bottle. I see Julia smooth back my mother's hair and hug her. I have never understood their friendship, when my mother is so cold and distant, and Julia is the opposite—warm and constant, a wall of love. Then the thought comes—they are just like Caplan and me. I disappear to the bathroom to check if I still need to cry, and everyone moves into the living room to play Wii *Just Dance*, another Caplan favorite.

When I come outside, he's there in the hallway.

"Hey," he says.

"Hi."

"You splashed water on your face. And your wrists."

"It's a little hot."

"Did you—you know? Were you having a moment, for a second, down there?"

"When?"

"When Quinn hugged you."

"Oh. I guess. A little. I'm fine now."

"Okay, good." He smiles. "You neverminded me, in the car, by the way. I didn't forget."

"I did," I sigh, "didn't I? Sorry."

"What happened?"

"I got embarrassed, that you thought—when I said that thing about belonging together—"

"I know," he says, "that was stupid. I was being stupid."

"I meant like . . . in life. We belong in each other's lives. I can't believe you thought I meant it like . . . like something other than, you know, just wanting things to stay like this."

"Like what?" he says.

I shrug. Our mothers both laugh, loud and free, as Quinn and Oliver begin their seminal classic dance to "It's Raining Men."

"Like this," I say, waving my hand toward the stairs.

"It will stay like this," he says. "I promise."

"Okay."

"You have to promise, too."

"You're the optimist," I say.

"Promise me, too, Mina."

"I promise," I say, rubbing a finger across my brow, "that if things do change, it will be for the better."

"Okay. I'll take it."

"Congratulations, Caplan."

"You, too!" he says, grinning, wicked.

"Oh, for what?"

"You got asked to prom!"

I shove him, and he shoves me, and we go back downstairs.

Our house feels quieter than normal after being at the Lewises', which is really saying something. I ask my mom if she wants one more cup of tea, but she tells me she's too tired. I decide to make her one anyway, with the idea of bringing it to her in bed and talking to her about Yale.

When I go to her room five minutes later, she's already asleep on top of the covers, still in her clothes. I decide to find a spare blanket, and for the first time in ten years, I open her closet.

Her old sundresses are all still there, in their candy-necklace colors. I can picture her, as through a telescope to another universe, teaching me dances with funny names when my father put his old music on. She with her ancient little boxes of obsolete library logs, and he with his record collection. I can't really picture his face beyond what I know from photos, but I can remember him laughing over the music while she and I would dance. I don't know why I have clearer memories of her from that time than of him. Maybe it is because her outline is still here, so I can see where all the old details are meant to go.

I remember waiting and waiting, while she drifted around our house in the blue-flowered nightgown, for her to put one of her sundresses on again, but she never did. One night, well after the funeral and all the fuss and attention had died down, when she was sleeping on the couch, still in the nightgown, I went into their closet to look at all her dresses, just to make sure they were real, and I hadn't imagined them. Of course, they hung fresh and clean and sad next to all his clothes. I think even then I realized that sooner or later some other grown-up would come in to manage all his things and erase his items, like the phantom books if the libraries had closed down, fallen out of use and left abandoned and forgotten and disappearing into whatever corner of the universe it is where leftover things go. So, I pulled down a few of his work shirts, with stiff collars and neat rows of small hard buttons, and hid them in my own closet, where at least their existence would be known by someone. Even if the someone was eight years old and the shirts went down below her knees.

Then, as if some unseen force were about to sweep through my life and wash all the technically useless items away, I gathered all the old borrowing cards my mother had given me from where they'd been proudly housed in a little box on my desk, and I hid them in the folds of his shirts.

I realize I've been standing in front of my mom's closet for so long that the tea's gotten cold. I pour it down the sink, bring up the blanket from the living room to cover her, and turn off her lights.

7

Caplan

After cake, I walk Mina and Ms. Stern home across the street, and then Quinn and I go to Pond Lake to smoke. He skates there to roll up while I walk behind him. He's in our usual spot when I get there, at the end of the eastern dock, where it's too dark to see from the shore.

Everyone knows the town is named for the two docks, but I learned in fourth grade why the lake is called Pond Lake, and of course, I learned it from Mina. It was the first anniversary of the day she lost her dad, and I remember feeling nervous, because I knew it should matter, but I didn't know how, and I didn't want to do or say anything to make it worse. I thought maybe I should give her privacy, but then my mom got home in the morning from her night shift with a store-bought blueberry pie. She said she was going to take it across the street to the Sterns. I remember asking her how she knew the pie wouldn't just remind them and make them more sad. She told me you can't remind people of something they never forget and always carry with them. And it is normal to be scared of other people's sadness and to pull away. But even if it isn't perfect, or if it's awkward, or if they hate pie, it's better to try. Better for them to know they aren't alone.

So, I crossed the street with her and just acted like it was any other Saturday. Mina was in the kitchen, eating a piece of toast. I remember it was the end of the loaf, that crappy bit no one really wants. She said her mom wasn't awake yet, so my mom cut us a piece each, put them on plates, and then took the entire rest of the thing upstairs and right into Mina's mom's room, with two forks, and no plates.

When we finished our slices and our moms hadn't come down yet, we decided to take a walk. It was cold that day for the first time that year, so I was surprised when we got to the lake and she walked out to the end of the western dock and sat. I could tell she'd been crying, and I didn't want to crowd her, so instead of following her, I walked around, picking my way along on the cool sand. I could see chimney smoke from one of the big houses set back on the south arc of the lake. I remember thinking summer left us too early that year.

I walked out on the eastern dock, sat across from her with the water between, and waited. It was impossible to think that the lake, with all its shifting and chang-ing shine, would freeze soon. I thought about watching Mina, the year before, ice-skating with her dad. I hoped she wasn't thinking the same. After a while, she stood and came around the lake, too. She grew small around the far side, stomping along with her hands in her jacket pockets, and then big again as she got close. She sat next to me. I couldn't think of something comforting to say, so I asked the first question that came to my mind.

"So, why d'ya think it's called Pond Lake?"

"I don't think. I know. I read it in a book about Two Docks."

She sounded a bit like she had a cold, and her nose was red, either from crying or the bite in the air, but I gave her a waiting look.

"All right. Well. In the nineteenth century—"

"What's a 'centry' again?"

"A *century* is one hundred years. A *sentry* is a soldier or a guard who protects a place."

"Oh, like, a bridge? Or a castle?"

"Do you want to learn about Pond Lake?"

"Yes," I said. "Sorry." I tried not to smile, because she sounded like Mina again.

"When Two Docks was becoming a town—"

"How does a town become a town?"

"Well, it already is one, and then it gets written down in a thing called a *charter*, and other people outside understand that it's real."

"But the people inside already know?"

"More or less," she said. "Can I keep going?"

"Yes."

"Well, when Two Docks was becoming a town, they realized Pond Lake needed a proper name, because the people in the town either called it the pond, or the lake, but two cartographers—"

"Cartographers?"

"Those are people who make maps."

"That's a job?"

"It is."

"Okay. Cool. I'd like that job, I think. Keep going."

"There were two cartographers, and they were great friends, and they set about naming Pond Lake. But before they could, they argued about whether it was actually a pond or a lake. They argued deep into the night—"

"Is that true, or are you making the story better?" I asked. She sighed, but I knew she was back from wherever she'd gone, on the western dock.

"This is what it said in the book. It's like a legend."

"All right."

"So the legend goes that they argued deep into the night. Then, just before dawn, they finally went to measure it. They walked around the outside, each starting at one dock, because that's how people used to measure distances, with their actual feet. It turned out it was more the size of a lake, but they couldn't dismiss that it had the distinct feeling of a pond."

"Huh. So it was both?"

"Yes. So the two cartographers argued and argued and then, as the sun rose, they tired of their argument. They didn't want to fight anymore, but they had not solved anything, and so they decided it would be a lake named Pond. Pond Lake."

"Pond Lake. Okay. That was a good story. Thanks."

"I think you'd make a good cartographer."

"How come?"

"You always know where you're going."

On my way around the lake to meet Quinn on the eastern dock, I pass some kids on a log who look around Ollie's age, reeking of pot.

"Be safe, boys," I say, trying to make them laugh, but they just stare at me.

"That's Cap Lewis," I hear one of them say once I've passed by.

Quinn is already smoking on the dock. He's taken his shoes and socks off and has his feet in the water. He's doctoring the joint. Quinn is amazing at rolling. It makes no sense, because his hands are huge and he has weird spider fingers, but he's always been good at things like that. He used to be obsessed with origami when we were younger. He'd rip off bits of his paper and fold them into tiny animals and line them up on his desk, all without ever looking away from the teachers, so they couldn't really get mad.

"That's disgusting," I say, looking at his feet, pale in the dark water.

"Come on, golden boy. You think your toes are too clean?"

I strip my shoes and socks off, too, and sit down next to him to take the joint.

"Did you see those little kids?" he asks.

"Yeah, they recognized me," I say.

"No shit."

"Yeah, as I walked away, they said, 'That's Cap Lewis.'"

He leans back. "Man, you really could be a much bigger asshole."

"It made me feel like one," I say.

"Oh, enjoy it. That's your life right now. You can do no wrong, you can have whatever you want, and then next year, you'll be at the bottom again."

"Don't say that," I say, passing him the joint. "We can't have whatever we want."

"Hey, can I ask you about something?"

Quinn has never, in the ten years that I've known him, asked me about something.

"What, did you kill someone?"

"Ha ha," he says, focusing carefully on fixing the joint, which is canoeing. He flicks his lighter a few times, but it doesn't catch. I hand him mine.

"So what's up?"

He watches the paper burn, curling and stubborn, not righting itself. He sighs. He takes a long hit.

"Mina looks different outside of school," he says.

"How so?" I ask. Not because I'm curious. I'm distracted, looking at the water moving over our ankles. Quinn and Mina only see each other outside of school accidentally, in passing, through me.

"She just looks different, like, with her hair back."

"Her hair back?"

"Like. Up. Off her face. You can actually see it."

I don't really know what to say to this, so I smoke more.

"She has a nice face," Quinn says, not looking at me.

"I've never really noticed," I say. "She kind of always looks the same to me."

Quinn nods.

We're quiet again. I think that it's all he wanted to say. And then:

"Do you think she'd go for me?"

I inhale way too much and start to cough. "Go for you?" I choke out.

"Like, get with me."

"Who?"

"Mina."

"With you?"

"Yeah, me."

"You and Mina?"

"Yeah, do you think?"

My throat feels raw and tight from coughing up smoke, and my eyes are watering. It takes me a second to get a response out. "Honestly, I don't think so. You know how she is. She's sort of, like, closed off."

"Yeah, but I feel like she's different around us," he says.

I feel annoyed that he lumped us together. That he thinks that he and I are the same, or even close. "And also, I don't think you're her type," I say.

"What's that mean?"

"Just that you guys are different. I don't know. She's also not your type."

"She's hot, that's my type," Quinn says, and we both start to laugh. It begins slow like an engine revving, and then we're both cackling, leaning into each other and gasping for breath, and everything's normal again.

"Mina is my fucking favorite person," I say, "but she's not hot."

"Dude, your eyes deceive you."

"She dresses like a Catholic schoolgirl."

"Caplan, that's literally porn."

"What the fuck?" We're both high and laughing so hard the conversation feels like nonsense. Like Dr. Seuss impossibleness.

"You're telling me you've never thought about it when she's up at the board in her schoolgirl skirt?"

"Jesus Christ, no," I say, still laughing. "No, I haven't. She's like my sister."

"Well, she's not mine."

"So . . . she like, lets her hair down, and now you like her?"

"I just told you, I like the way her hair looks up," he says.

"So what?"

"*So* . . . should I go for it?"

"Sure," I say. "Your funeral."

"Don't be a dick. I'm asking if you'd be cool with it."

"Yeah, of course. I'm not, like, in charge of that. It's up to her, not me." I bite the inside of my cheek at the idea. I can just imagine her face if he tried to lean in, looking at him like he's out of his mind. Which he is.

"I know," he says. "But you know what I mean."

"I don't."

"You guys sort of belong to each other."

I shake my head. I pass him the joint.

"Not like that," he says, taking it, smiling at something across the water. "But yeah. In a way."

His phone rings.

"It's Hollis," he says, looking down. He picks it up on speaker. "Hey, Hol."

"Hey, what's up?" she says.

"I'm with Cap at the lake."

She doesn't say anything for a second.

"Why? What's up?" Quinn asks.

She laughs into the phone. "I was just gonna ask you if he was okay. He, like, ran from my car today like his house was on fire or something, and then hasn't answered any of my texts."

"Oh, fuck," I say, opening my own phone.

"Caplan is very sorry for being an idiot golden retriever," says Quinn, "and he's typing an apology now."

"Thanks, Quinn. You're my bitch."

"Am not."

"Yes, you are. Say you're my bitch."

"I'm your bitch." He hangs up.

"Goddamn it," I say. I can feel Hollis looking at our messages, watching the little typing icon next to my name, laughing at me. She had in fact texted me a few times, once during school, something funny about the condom, once to ask if I was okay, and then once more, calling me a douche.

"Are you having second thoughts?" Quinn asks.

"No, not at all. I just got distracted," I say. "What do I say?"

"Just say you forgot about her."

"I can't fucking say I forgot about her."

"Then just go over and throw rocks at her window."

"It's almost midnight."

"So?"

"We have school tomorrow."

"Oh, come on, man," he says, standing up and offering me his hand. "We're seniors. We're victory lapping. We're in a movie. Go act like it."

Ten minutes later, I'm standing on Hollis's front lawn, and I call her. She picks up.

"Hi, Cap."

"Quinn said to throw pebbles. But I'm being a pussy."

I see the light in her room turn on. She opens the window. "Well?"

"Hi."

"Hi."

"I'm sorry I didn't text you back."

"You shouldn't be allowed to have a phone. You're a waste of a plan."

"I'm just better in person," I say. "This digital age, the overlord screens, the unreality of our modern world—"

"Please shut up."

"Are you gonna come get me?"

"Come around the back."

I make my way up her driveway, sticking close to the house so I won't set off the motion sensor lights. She opens the basement door, the screen hitting the side of her house with a soft click. It reminds me of summer, of sneaking out in middle school, of freshman year, stumbling out and smacking it open just like that, to throw up in the garden. I'd run out in the middle of her giving me a blow job for the first time because we'd shotgunned beers upstairs right before. Hollis is weirdly good at shotgunning.

"Hi," I say again.

She shushes me and pulls me inside. "Are you high?"

"No. Yes. A little."

"You're going to make my bed smell like weed."

"Should I not have come?"

"No." She puts her hands on her hips. "No. I'm glad you came. You look sweet."

"Sweet?"

"Funny. Handsome."

"You look pretty," I say. She does.

"Why are you holding your socks?"

"We put our feet in the water."

"Gross. Come on, lost boy."

"What, are you not gonna do the dock jump before grad?"

"Fair point." She leads me quietly up the carpeted basement steps and then the terrifying wooden staircase in her front hall that always creaks. We pass her school photos, framed in a train alongside her siblings', marching up the wall. I pause as she tugs on my arm, and I take a photo of a photo, zooming in too much—Hollis in a ballerina outfit and a crown, holding roses, no front teeth.

We have sex in her shower, which is always how we do it when her parents are home, and then we get straight into her bed before we're dry, which I know she normally hates, but she's being nice.

"Are you not gonna comb your hair?" I whisper. She always combs her hair after showering. I've never seen it all wet and tangled before.

"Mm," she says, "too sleepy."

"Want me to do it?"

She opens her eyes. "Do you know how?"

"I've watched you do it a hundred times," I say, taking her comb from the nightstand. "Here, sit up."

She does, tucking her knees under her chin, and I sit behind her with my legs on either side of her and comb, starting at the ends, like she always does.

"You're gonna be a really good dad," she says out of nowhere.

I'm glad she can't see my face. "I doubt it," I say, "if I take after mine."

"You won't," she says. "I hope you have a daughter. That's how sure I am that you'll be good."

I'm still combing, even though her hair is smooth. It's a good high activity, repetitive and peaceful. She opens my phone and looks at the picture of her as a little kid that I took on the stairs.

"Wanna make that my background?" I ask.

She gives me a look over her shoulder.

"What? Is that corny?"

"Yes," she says, and she does it, pressing her mouth into her knees, the phone light cool and blue on her face.

I stay till she falls asleep.

8

Mina

On Friday, Caplan skips biology to spend my study hall with me in the library. He says it's so he can study for his Spanish final, which is later that day. The irony of skipping to study is lost on him.

"I'm randomly fire at biology," he says, "but I can, like, barely pass English, which is my first language, so."

"You still shouldn't be skipping," I say. "Can't you study at lunch?"

"No, cause it's Hollis's birthday."

"I thought the party was tonight?"

"Yeah, but the girls are, like, bringing balloons to school or something. It'll be a whole thing if I'm not there."

"Okay, but you don't need me. I don't speak Spanish."

"I study better with you sitting there," he says. "What? Am I intruding on you reading *Pride and Prejudice* for the tenth time?"

I ignore him. Once he goes back to his index cards, I look up.

He's staring at one like he's trying to see straight through it, with his tongue sticking out a tiny bit.

"You're making the face."

He groans, drops his flash cards in a pile, and shoves them toward me, flattening himself out on the table.

"I'm gonna fail."

"You're not gonna fail."

"Okay, I'm not gonna fail, but I have a seventy-nine in this class, so it would be really sick to get, like, an A."

"I don't think it matters at this point," I say.

"Are you not studying for finals, then?"

I narrow my eyes.

He goes back to his flash cards, and I go back to my book. It's *Emma*, not *Pride and Prejudice*, but I wasn't as into it.

I feel more than I see someone looking at us from across the room.

"That girl just took a photo of us," I say.

Caplan looks up and waves at the girl like he's the goddamned mayor of the library.

"That's Ruby," he says. "You know Ruby. She's probably just taking photos for yearbook committee."

I do know her, as one of Hollis's minions, but they spend enough time pretending to forget my name, so. Privately, I'm positive that photo was taken to send in a group chat with all those girls to talk about me. I try to return to my book, but can't stop thinking about how ugly it's possible to look from that distance. Phones have good zoom these days. And I have a zit I picked on my chin. Now it's a scab and looks much worse than it did as a zit.

"Want me to read over your final history paper?" I say.

He looks up. His hair's standing straight up from all the times he's run his fingers through it.

"That," he says, "would be amazing. You don't mind?"

"No, I'm bored. Hand it over."

He makes a face.

"What?"

"Okay, honestly, I haven't started."

"Cool, it's definitely due Monday."

"I was wondering if you'd maybe help me, like, outline it?"

"Nope. I'll read it over when you're done."

"Meen—"

"At like, three a.m. on Sunday night, probably, because I'm a giver."

"The bubonic plague just like—doesn't do anything for me."

"I don't think the bubonic plague did it for anyone," I say.

"Just one tiny seed of one of your extra ideas," he says. "Come on, I know you had like ten."

"I did not," I say, "cause it was an awful topic. But even if I did, I wouldn't give them to you, because I will not do your homework for you. We're both better than that."

"You are. I'm not," he huffs, sliding down on his seat. "It would just be more expedient."

"Good word, *expedient.*"

"It's my word of the day."

I look up from my book. "Your word of the day?"

"Yes. I have an app."

"An app that gives you a word for the day?"

"Yes. I downloaded it to better my vocabulary so you'll never get bored of talking to me."

"You're ridiculous."

"You used to be way cooler about cheating. Remember when you would sell book reports in elementary school?"

"How could I forget. My most popular moment to date. And that wasn't real cheating."

"It so was," he says, shaking his head. "And you profited off it. Fifty cents a pop."

"I always made sure you guys had read the book. I would just do the writing part. I felt like I was helping as long as you were all actually reading."

"Hey, no need to defend yourself. If you're going to hell, I'll see you there," he says.

"I'll be near the snacks."

"I never understood how you knew if we had read our books or not," he says then, leaning his chair back on two legs.

"I would ask you guys questions."

"Yes, but you had to have read all the books we read. It was amazing. It was like you read every single book in the elementary school library."

"Not true. I actually had to read *Pretty Little Liars* for Hollis."

He laughs, slamming back down onto four legs. "I forgot about that!"

"I didn't. It gave me nightmares for weeks. I was really scared of the blind girl."

"Ableist."

"She was only pretending to be blind, so that's actually—whatever. Never mind."

"No neverminds—"

"She was scary as shit. That's all."

"But you read it?"

"Yeah, all twenty-three of them," I say. "Cause Hollis was scarier, even then."

"Yeah, I remember." He smiles. "Twenty-three, jeez. She had you whipped."

"Hollis has us all whipped."

"You're telling me," he says. Then: "Okay. Speaking of. I have to ask you for something."

"Yes?"

"It's sort of a favor."

"All right."

"I know you said you weren't gonna go to Hollis's birthday thing tonight—"

"Caplan, it wasn't a real invitation."

"No, it was," he says. "She brought it up again."

"What do you mean?"

"Like she said she hoped you would come. And I said you probably thought she meant it as a joke—"

"Yeah, cause she did—" I say.

"And then she asked if you thought she was that big of a bitch—"

"Good grief." I put my head in my hands.

"And then she asked if *I* thought she was a bitch—"

"Of course she did."

"And so," he sighs, plunging on, "I said that I'd been wrong, and you were probably really touched and excited to come."

"Did you, now."

"Yeah. And then she got all pleased."

"What, is she planning to dump pig's blood on me?"

"Is that a reference? I don't get it."

"It's from *Carrie*."

"Carrie who?"

"Never mind."

"No never—"

"Cap. What are you asking me for?"

"I think she, like, wants you to come. I think she's trying to be nice. Come on, don't raise your eyebrows like that. And I—yeah, I, too, think it would be fun if you came."

"Caplan, why—"

"Because parties are fun. You're fun. I don't get why you have such an aversion to them."

"You should watch *Carrie*."

"Is it because of your smell thing? With alcohol?"

"No," I say, starting to feel really irritated. "I'm over that. You've seen me around alcohol. We had champagne last night."

"So then come!" He does his unfair face, all dimples, and lays himself out on the table again, hanging on to both my upper arms as I cross them. "Please?"

He sits up suddenly, pulling his hands back.

"Quinn will be happy, too."

"Why would Quinn care?"

"He kind of told me he likes you."

I stare at him.

He stares back. He shrugs.

"Likes me?"

"Like, *like* likes."

"Are you five years old?"

"Come on. Don't shoot the messenger."

"That. That is so dumb, I'm not even dignifying it with a response," I say.

"People want you around."

"*You* want me around."

"True," he says, "I do. So will you come?"

"I will consider it."

"Fantastic. Thank you."

I go to mark my page, but it's already folded down, because I haven't read more than a sentence. "Did Quinn really say something about me?"

"Ooooh," he says, standing and cramming the flash cards into his bag. "Now she's curious. Guess you'll have to show up tonight to find out."

"You shouldn't just shove shit into your bag. It's a mess."

"You're a mess." He ruffles my hair.

"You're being weird today," I say. "You high-fived the crossing guard earlier."

"I'm in a good mood," he says, following me out of the library. "Sue me. It smelled like summer this morning. And we're going to a party tonight."

On my way out of the house that night, my mother stops me, which is unusual.

"Where are you off to?"

"Hanging out with Caplan."

"Is it a date?"

"Mom. Why would you even ask that?"

She's at the top of the stairs, looking down at me. "You just look nice, that's all. I was wondering why you're dressed up."

"I'm not dressed up."

"All right, Mina." She sighs and touches the spot above her left eye. She turns to go back to her bedroom.

"I'm going to a party," I say.

"Oh?"

"Yes. With Caplan's friends. It's his girlfriend's birth-day."

She smiles at me in this odd way.

I glare back.

"That's nice of them to include you," she says, coming down the stairs. "I remember that happening at the end of high school, people stop caring so much about who's popular or who's in the clique."

"Wow, thanks, Mom."

"Oh no, I'm sorry. I didn't mean—"

I cut her off with a hug. She feels small in my arms, thinner than I am, but she clutches me back.

"I was just teasing," I say into her hair. "I know I'm not Miss High School."

"I kinda like you, though," she says, tugging on my braid. "But why don't you wear your contacts?"

"Okay, now I'm leaving."

"You just look so lovely with your hair back!"

"Good-bye, Mom! Love you!"

"Why hide your face?"

"If I don't wear glasses," I say from the door, "then they will really know I'm trying."

"It's not so bad to try," she says.

"I could say the same to you." I give the tie of her robe a little yank. It makes her laugh. It surprises us both. She looks then like she's about to cry. Instead, she says—

"We should make sure you have a new pair you love. For next fall."

.   .   .

I think, even when my dad was here, she was the more introverted half of the pair. Opposites attract and all that. Now, her only real friend is Julia, and that's just because Julia refused to give up on her and had the advantage of proximity. A long time ago, somewhere in the valley between the blue-flowered nightgown and wherever she lives today, I remember she would have these strange bursts of manic energy. She'd emerge as if from underwater, gasping for air. She was like a time traveler, waking suddenly with no idea what year it was. I remember a mommy-and-me music class that I was humiliatingly too old for. She left me there halfway through the first session, and I found her weeping in the bathroom. I remember a mother-daughter book club with some of her old work colleagues that we joined and never attended. And then, of course, the annual family vacation with my dad's old friends from Yale. All those kids around my age. The grown-up father versions of the laughing young men who put her on their shoulders on the dance floor in their wedding photos. I have strange, beautiful memories of those trips from when he was alive, fragmented and distant through a kaleidoscope, being wrapped up with other tiny bodies in one gigantic, bright, striped beach towel, snug and together, to fall asleep on the sand. Someone else's mother putting sunscreen on my nose.

After he died, they continued to invite us each year. Each year, she would mention it, and I wouldn't dare let myself hope. Each year, the days between Christmas and New Year's came and went, and the trip with it, while we stayed home. I can't think why they kept at it, reaching out to us, when she ignored them for so many years. Either they felt sorry for us, or whatever brotherhood was forged in my dad's freshman year dorm was built to extend beyond anything, past death, through generations, and across families. When I was thirteen, the invitation coincided with one of her erratic surges of life, and so, after five years of social isolation, we went with them to Turks and Caicos. The trip, suffice it to say, did not go well.

She adjusts the tie of her robe and steps away from me, backing up the stairs.

"Go have fun, then, you disrespectful partying teenager," she says.

Once I'm out of the house, I check my phone. I have a text from Caplan—

> don't kill me but I went over early to help set up

I start to type, then stop. We planned to walk to Hollis's together. But it is so fair, so reasonable of him, to go early to his own girlfriend's birthday party, and so unfair and unreasonable of me to be incapable of walking into a party, walking into any room ever, without him, that I kick the curb. It really hurts. I sit down and hold my foot as my eyes water, feeling like a fool in my mother's mascara and a sundress from tenth grade. He texts me again.

> ur not bailing, I'm coming to get you

I respond:

> Don't do that, it's fine.

so ur coming?

I don't answer for a moment.

i'll come meet you out front when you get here

9
Caplan

Hollis is happiest when she's hosting. I told her this once, and she said she just loves attention and being the best at something. My first real memory of her was in her backyard, at a party.

It's a backyard meant for sledding, a corner house, with a long, gentle slope. When we were younger, she used to host everyone each year for the first big snow. All her siblings would invite friends, kids in their classes, kids on the block, and they called it the sledding carnival. The first time, we must have been nine or ten. I remember I thought it was strange to be going to hang out at a girl's house, but Quinn convinced me to go because he'd overheard Hollis on the playground describing how it felt to sled on her lawn. She'd said it was like flying. There was hot chocolate on the porch and more Christmas lights than I'd ever seen in one place. I remember the lights and the trees and the marshmallows and the back of Hollis's head, long strawberry braids sticking out of a blue knit cap, flying ahead of me on a sled, fast as a blizzard, as childhood, fresh and bright and sharp like the first time you realize girls are so pretty.

Tonight the air is warm and heavy, and she's turning eighteen. When I come around the side of the house, I see her balancing on a stool trying to hang a paper lantern, blowing a bit of hair out of her face, in my TDHS track T-shirt and cutoffs. Out of nowhere, I feel really fond of her, and then also sort of sad, but I can't tell why. When she sees me she smiles, then groans, and holds her hand out to me. I put her on my shoulders to help her hang the rest, her thighs sticking to the sides of my neck in the heat. When we're done, the lanterns stretch in a swoop from the top of their tree house down to the porch railing. We go inside for her to change and to have sex.

The sun sets as everyone arrives and the lanterns get brighter. The firepit's going and some of the boys are playing beer die on the big piece of plywood she's had set across two stools for most of high school for just that purpose. Quinn has to leave early because he still does community service on Friday nights, but just before he does, we flip the plywood together to reveal his present. I've been helping him out, letting him know when Hollis and I were off somewhere together, so he could paint the bottom in secret. Now it's green and gold and says TWO DOCKS HIGH SCHOOL CLASS OF 2016, and beneath that in more gold, A TOAST TO THE HOST: LONG LIVE THE QUEEN. Around the letters is a rough map of our town, all the places we live, Two Docks High, the lower schools, Little Bend River, Orben and Sons' diner, Pond Lake, all our spots. It was an awesome moment, seeing her face when we flipped it, but Quinn was the only one who could have painted it, with massive graffiti and perfectly clean lines. I realize I should have gotten her something else, too.

After she takes a thousand pictures of it, she goes and gets a bag of Sharpies and asks people to sign their names inside the white block letters. She checked with Quinn first before he left, and he told her she could dance on it till it snapped in half if she wanted to. It was hers. When I sign it, I write *happy birthday top girl, love Cap.* I take some shit for it, but I don't really care.

When Mina calls me, I go to meet her in the driveway. She looks so tense, with her arms crossed over her bag, that I have the instinct to take her hand or something just to make her uncoil, but that wouldn't do any good. We walk in, and I wish Quinn were already back, cause he's so good at making her laugh, but Hollis calls out to me and waves us over.

"Your backyard looks so beautiful," Mina says, looking up at the lanterns.

"Come, look what Quinn did!" Hollis pulls Mina to the table, a bit bossy, but unlocking her posture all the same. Everyone is setting up flip cup, and Hollis makes them all pause so Mina can sign the table.

"There," says Hollis, "now we've got everyone," and Mina actually smiles. She pulls a book out of her bag.

"You brought a book?" Becca says.

I hate Becca.

"Um." Mina looks around at everyone and then down at the book. "It's for you." She holds it out toward Hollis, who is staring at it like she'd never seen one before. "It's from Caplan," Mina says quickly. "He chose it. I just picked it up from Dusty's."

"He forgot it there, didn't he?" she says, rolling her eyes.

They both laugh, and suddenly everything is very normal.

"We could mark the trail of your lost items on this map," Hollis says, pointing down at the table. "It spans the town."

"Oh, I think the Michigan news just distracted him," Mina says.

"Michigan?" Hollis looks at Mina and then at me.

My heart falls into my ass. I desperately try to remember when I told Hollis I got into Michigan. I must have told her. How could I not have told her?

"You got in?"

"Yeah," I say, "I totally thought I—" And then she hugs me.

"Congratulations," she says into my neck. I'm so relieved that I kiss her.

Becca, still looking sullen, tries to pull Hollis away to take a shot, but Hollis stays put, and they have a very fast, furious silent argument.

Becca turns to Mina. "Right, also, Mina, I wanted to say sorry for being a bitch this week in the hallway," she says.

"Oh?"

"When I brought up the puppy dog joke. I thought I was being funny, but, yeah. I wasn't."

"Don't worry about it," Mina says. "We're all feeling nostalgic."

"Exactly, totally!"

Hollis, looking pleased, winks at me and then goes to put the book safely inside.

"So what book did I choose specially?" I whisper to Mina as she drifts back to me.

"It's called *My Brilliant Friend.*"

"Fitting."

"I'm sorry, I panicked. I thought everyone would bring her presents, and then I felt weird, and—"

"No, you saved my ass. I didn't really get her anything."

She shakes her head at me.

"And I have no idea how I forgot to tell her about Michigan."

"Do you enjoy flying so close to the sun?"

"Everyone does," I say. "Isn't that the point of that story?" I step up quickly to flip my cup and drink my beer and then fall back again. "So what's the puppy dog joke?"

"Oh, I don't even remember."

It's close to a nevermind, but I let it go, because she still looks on edge. "It's good that you came," I say instead. "It made her happy, I can tell."

"I can't believe Quinn put my house on that map," she says.

"Course he did. Can't do mine without yours."

"Where is he, anyway?"

"Oh, he's at his community service. He'll be back soon."

"It's a really wonderful gift," she says, looking down at the table.

"Yeah. I mean, I helped," I say. "I got her out of the house and stuff."

Then someone stops the music, and two of the girls come down the back porch steps with a cake. Everyone sings for Hollis, who beams around at us all, the only person I've ever met who knows just what to do with themselves when they get sung "Happy Birthday." Mina gives me a little push, and I go to stand with her. Hollis kisses me and then closes her eyes and takes her time wishing. After she blows out her candles, everyone cheers. Someone calls out asking her what she wished for.

"Don't answer," I say into her ear. "Fuck 'em. Keep your wish."

She takes the handle of vodka sitting on the table, holds it up to us all, and says, "For six more months of June!"

Someone's shaken up a bottle of champagne and starts spraying us. She takes a pull and passes the vodka to me. They turn the music back on, and everyone is dancing and hugging each other, even Mina.

"TAKE A KNEE!" one of the boys shouts, and he goes around pouring the vodka into people's mouths. Hollis is kissing me, dripping and sticky with champagne, and I open my eyes just in time to see Mina. It happens so quickly, everyone banging into each other and passing between us. Someone holds the bottle out to her, an arm thrust from the mess of people, connected to no one. She shakes her head, and maybe they don't see or don't realize, but they don't stop the arc of their arm, raising the bottle, tipping it, and Mina is shrinking away with her mouth clamped, blocked in by the people behind her.

Then she is soaking wet. So is everyone, so am I, and everyone is laughing and dancing, but I see her face turn. I pull away from Hollis and get to Mina one second before her knees give out. She's hyperventilating. People start to realize.

I half carry her to the house. People turn to look, in

slow drunk time. Hollis comes running after us, asking what's wrong. I ignore her.

As soon as we're inside, Mina starts to sob. I carry her down the stairs to the basement, where there's a bathroom with a shower. When I turn on the water, she comes back to me a little. She's still breathing too fast and shallow, but she takes off her glasses, turns the water hotter, and tells me to go.

"I'll stay."

"Go, I've got it."

"Mina."

"Please go back to the party." Her back is to me. "Please go act normal."

I sit outside against the bathroom door, listening to the water, trying to hear if she's crying.

10

Mina

I am thirteen and it's too dark to see, or maybe my eyes are shut. I'm on a hotel bed. Who knows how many people have lain here before me. I can't move, because there's something heavy on top of me. The air smells sharp.

I am eighteen and I am belonging, for the first time. The air smells sharp again, but I hold myself still inside, breathe through my mouth, and try to take in all the other things. Golden globes bobbing in an indigo sky, tall pink candles in white icing, how love looks, messy and bright. Someone tries to grab my arm and swing me around in a dance, but I need my arms to hold myself together. Then I am covered in the burning smell. I close my eyes and try to go inside of myself, but that's always the mistake I make.

. . .

I am thirteen and it's too dark to see and I can't move.
There is someone heavy on top of me. Who knows how
many people have lain still before me.

Then I'm burning my skin away. Making myself clean.
Making myself my own. I'm alone, but I know where I
am now, and I know Caplan is nearby.

"How long has it been?"
    "Like nothing. Twenty minutes. Can I touch you?"
    I shake my head.
    He hands me the towel.
    "I'm sorry," I say.
    "Don't say sorry." He takes me up through the house
and out the front door. I sit down on the curb feeling
shaky, and cold, and a bit stupid.
    "I'm—"
    "Please don't say sorry again, Mina."
    "Well, I am."
    "No. I'm sorry. I made you come."
    "Well, that's stupid. No one bullied me. I didn't get
pig's blood dropped on me."
    "Yeah, just vodka."
    "It was fun. Everyone was being fun. I ruined it."
    We sit. I can still hear the party.
    "That hasn't happened to me in so long," I say.
    "Was it the smell?"
    "Yeah, I guess." I put my head down between my
knees.
    "Can I touch you?"

"Yes," I say to the ground. "I'm fine now."

He puts his hand on my back, rubbing it in wide circles. "Can I ask something?"

"Sure."

"Is this why you don't want to go to Yale? Cause it happened on the trip you guys took with those Yale families?"

"I don't know. Well. Yeah, he still goes there."

Caplan's hand stops moving on my back.

"He's only a junior. So he'll be there next year."

"I thought. You never said." Caplan's voice sounds strange and thin. It scares me. I finally look at him. "You never told me you knew him," he says. "I thought he was a stranger. Just some random person staying at the same hotel."

"I didn't know him that well," I say. "But yeah, one of those kids. That's why he walked me back to my room. That's how—yeah. Don't look at me like that. You're going to make me cry."

He doesn't seem to be able to speak.

"Don't you dare fucking cry, Caplan."

He wraps his arms around me. Eventually, I let my head rest on his shoulder. If it weren't for Caplan, I don't know how or when I'd have learned to let people touch me again.

"Their fucking Christmas card is on our fridge right now," I say, and then I start to laugh.

"Oh my god, Mina."

"It's funny."

"How is that funny?"

But he lets me laugh myself out. When I'm done, he says, "Why'd you even apply? If you knew he was there?"

"I didn't think I'd get in."

Then he lets me cry myself out.

"I know everyone thought I was delusional when I didn't apply to more schools. But I told you. Michigan wasn't a backup." I'm glad my head's on his shoulder, so he can't see my face. "I just want to go where you go."

"I wish neither of us had to go anywhere."

I hear the rake of wheels on gravel. Quinn comes soaring toward us, slipping off the board and scooping it up.

"Hey!" he calls out.

Caplan doesn't reply, so I do, shifting away from him. "Hi, Quinn."

"You guys okay?" He peers down at us in the dark.

"Yeah, we're good," Caplan says.

"Okay," says Quinn, "because the girls are all standing back there in the driveway, whispering and looking down here like it's a crime scene."

"Yeah, I was about to walk Mina home," Caplan says.

"No," I say, standing. "The party's not over. Go be with Hollis."

"It's fine. Come on—"

"Don't be dumb. You can't leave."

"Stop it," he says. "I'm walking you home."

"I can walk myself home."

"I know you can, I just—"

"I can walk Mina home?"

We both look at Quinn.

"I mean," he says, putting one hand into his pocket and kicking a sneaker into the curb. "Yeah, if you'd want?"

His shoulders pinch up and his eyebrows are raised. He looks nervous. I've never seen Quinn look nervous. It makes me want to laugh again. I feel bizarre. Funny and light, like I'm floating.

"You just got here, though."

"Yeah, but just to check if you were still here. Ah, yeah, you and Cap. So if you're leaving, it's on my way. Kinda."

"Okay," I say.

"Are you sure?" Caplan asks me. He's also looking nervous. "I'm not gonna sleep here. I'll come say hey when I get home—"

"No, stay here," I say, folding the towel up and handing it to him. "And tell Hollis I'm sorry I left. And sorry about—yeah, just wish her a happy birthday again for me."

"All right," he says. He stands there holding the towel. Once Quinn and I set off down the street, he turns back up the driveway.

"So," Quinn says. "Why the fuck are you all wet?"

"Oh. It's a long, boring story."

"Same story as why Caplan was looking at you like that?"

"Like what?"

"Like you're a baby bird?"

"Yeah. I don't know."

"Do you, like," he says, "wanna talk about it?"

"Um."

"You don't have to, either—"

"No, that's okay—"

"It's not my business—" We talk over each other. I'm still feeling very strange. Not in a bad way, for once.

"It's really okay. It was not a big deal, I just got anxious," I say.

"Like, more anxious than usual?"

"Are you making fun of me?"

"A little, yeah," he says, lips creeping up. "Can't help it. But also just asking."

"Someone spilled vodka on me. I freaked out, and then I had to get into the shower because that sometimes calms me down. So that's why I'm all wet."

"Totally," says Quinn. "Makes sense."

"Does it?"

"Sure." He shrugs. "Everyone's got their weird shit."

"I don't think other people's shit makes them lose it and ruin parties."

"Oh, I doubt you ruined the party."

"I definitely embarrassed myself."

"Well, just last week," he says, "in that very backyard, I'd been drinking all day and tried to hit the bong and then I vomited all over the driveway in front of everyone."

"That's disgusting."

"Feel better, though?" he asks. He walks suddenly under the beam of a streetlight.

"Yeah. I do, actually."

"Remember in fourth grade when Mr. Grant wouldn't let me fold my pieces of paper while taking a test, and I flipped my desk over and got sent to the principal's office?"

"I do."

"See?"

"What's your point? Everyone will remember this forever?"

"Nope. That everyone's got shit."

"Thanks, Quinn."

"No problem, Mina."

"And thanks for walking me home."

"It's cool."

"And thanks for asking me to prom. Even if that was also you making fun of me."

"You keep thanking me for things I wanted to do," he says.

I look sideways at him. His profile is harsh in the light of a car that comes swinging around the corner. We hop up onto the curb, and he touches the small of my back with his hand quickly before dropping it. A wave rolls in my stomach. I wonder if I'm going to go to pieces again. I will myself not to. I have the feeling that something good is, for the first time in my life, happening to me and that I don't want to miss it. Not something too big or terrible, not a nightmare, not a tragedy, just a nice, normal something. Immediately after having this thought, I feel ridiculous. A person is just walking me home. Just a boy. Just Quinn.

When we were little, Quinn was the loudest and the messiest. He colored on walls and broke things and spilled every cup he touched. He used to have ears that stuck out and pointy little features. A shock of dark hair. I couldn't take two steps without him sticking out his foot to trip me. I couldn't answer a question in class without him snickering. I used to think he looked like an evil little elf. I shake myself.

"Are you shivering?" Quinn asks.

"No, I'm fine."

"You have goose bumps!"

"I don't—"

"You do, and your dress is still wet."

I look down. My dress is wet. It is also see-through.

"Here—" He starts to take off his sweatshirt. His T-shirt comes with it, pulling away from the waist of his jeans, a strip of red plaid boxers. He has abs.

"I'm fine!" I shriek. I pull his arms down.

"Okay, okay!" He's laughing. "I take it back."

"Take what back?"

"My middle school flirting."

"You are not flirting with me," I say.

"I kind of was."

We walk in silence. I try desperately to think of something to say. *After the next streetlight,* I tell myself, *I will say something. At the next corner, I will say something.*

"Okay, I'm sorry," he says. "I'll never offer you my sweatshirt again."

"It's not that. We're just so close to my house."

"We'd get there sooner if we skated," he says, sounding evil again.

"I can't skate."

"I bet you've never tried."

"I couldn't even stand on that thing."

"You could absolutely stand on it." He drops the board down between us. "Come on."

"Quinn."

"Just stand. On a still board."

He takes my hands. I step up.

"See. Super easy." He starts to walk slowly, still holding both my hands.

"Okay, now *this* is middle school flirting."

"No," he says, moving faster, "this is skating."

I let us go a few feet, clinging to Quinn too hard for it to be cute. My hands feel sweaty. I can't look at him, so I look down at my legs, all wrong and awkward, knees knocked, and his sneakered feet, sidestepping, one crossing over the other with surprising grace, the street slipping past beneath us.

"Okay, I'm done." I jump off, stumbling, and he runs after the board.

"You're a natural," he says, jogging back to me.

"You're an idiot." I cross my arms back over my chest. We're almost at my house. I feel disappointed. We fall back into step.

"So how was community service?" I ask. Boring. Boring fucking question.

"It was good. I just teach a class at the rec center."

"You teach a class?"

"Yeah, I guess it's not technically community service anymore. Like, I finished my required time."

"When?"

"Um, ninth grade? Or eighth, I forget. So now it's just a job, I guess."

"What do you teach?"

"Ah," he laughs nervously, swinging his free arm. "Sewing?"

"You can sew?"

"Sure," he says. "I made this little guy." He points to the small tree on his baseball cap.

We're in front of my house now.

"Quinn, that's like—embroidery."

"I guess," he says. "Don't tell anyone."

We stand there facing each other.

"You teach an embroidery class at the rec on Friday nights?"

"Yeah," he says, "mostly to ten-year-old girls. And two really neat old ladies."

He's looking at me like he's balanced on an edge, waiting for the wind to tip him. Something comes loose inside of me. I kiss him. Or I try. I press my mouth against his. His hat falls off. Then I run inside without looking back.

11

Caplan

I know as soon as they walk off that it was a mistake, abandoning Mina to Quinn when she was still so shaky. I also know it would be wrong to walk Mina home just to avoid facing Hollis. I press the heels of my hands into my eyes and head back up the driveway. My head swims. A few of the girls stand at the gate, not even pretending they aren't talking about me. In the backyard, there are still some people left, smoking around the fire. I see Hollis moving around in her house through the kitchen windows.

She doesn't look up when I come in the back door. She stacks sticky Solo cups, pouring extra beer down the sink.

"Want help?"

"It's okay, I'm almost done."

"Hollis." I slide down against the cabinets, rubbing my head again. "I'm really sorry."

"It's okay."

"Mina needed me. It's hard to explain."

"You don't have to explain."

"Please don't be mad," I say. "Or if you are, just yell and get it over with. This is worse."

"Caplan. What kind of person do you think I am?"

"What?"

"Of course I'm not mad."

"You're not?"

"No. I've seen a panic attack before, you know."

"Oh."

"Will she be okay?"

"Yeah," I say. "Quinn's walking her home now."

"That's nice of him." She sits down next to me on the floor. "Cap, why didn't you tell me you got into Michigan?"

"I don't even know. I forgot. I'm sorry."

"Is that where you went when you left the car? To tell Mina?"

"Um, no, I went to open the email with her."

Hollis shakes her head. She smiles, but she looks so sad, too. I open my mouth to say I don't even know what, when she says—

"Do you want to stay?"

"Really, can I?"

She stands and pulls me to my feet. With her head against my chest, she says, "Can you kick everyone out now so we can just go to bed?"

I nod again, my chin hitting the top of her head. "You're really not mad?"

"No, I'm not mad."

"Then why are you being so quiet?" I ask.

"I'm just tired," she says.

.   .   .

After the dance of thanking her parents, saying good-bye, leaving through the front, and coming in again around back, we lie together in her room. She's tucked into my side, so I can't see her.

"Thanks again for understanding. And thanks for including Mina."

"I'm sorry it was such a disaster," she says. "Hopefully, it'll be better next time."

"Next time?"

"I've decided if she's your friend, she's mine, too."

"Really? That's—that's so great—"

"And I've decided not to compete with her anymore."

I don't know what to say to that. "I can't believe you told everyone your wish."

"Oh, I don't need it to come true."

"What do you mean?"

She rolls over to face me, thinking, her hands pressed together under her cheek. "I felt that way looking at everyone, just for a second. That I want senior spring to last forever. But it was just a second. I don't actually want that at all."

"You don't?"

"No, of course not. I want to get the fuck out of here. We're outgrowing it."

"You think?"

"Yeah. Don't you?"

"I don't know. I hadn't thought about it."

"That's you," she says. "You'll sail right along like nothing's ending and then forget to say good-bye."

"Good-bye, Holly," I mumble, my eyes closing.

"I can't wait to be in New York City. I'm gonna be the least cool person there."

"Why would you want that?"

"I can adapt. Just think how cool I'll end up."

"You'll want nothing to do with me," I say.

"It's for the best."

"Hey," I say.

"What, you want me to end up Mrs. Hollis Lewis?"

"God, that sounds bad. We can't do that. That's terrible. What are we gonna do?"

She's quiet for a second, but I can tell she's smiling into her hands.

"I think about it a lot, actually. I love my name. I don't want to change it, but I also want to have the same name as my whole family someday."

"Hollis Cunningham," I say. "It's a good name."

"Maybe I'll do what your mom did. Name my son Cunningham, and take my husband's last name."

"As long as it sounds good," I say, pulling her closer. "You can marry someone else, as long as they have a better last name."

"Okay, deal," she says.

"Hey, Hollis," I whisper.

"Hi, Cap."

"Happy birthday."

I wake up at 5:00 a.m., a little hungover, with a bad hollow feeling in my gut. Hollis is still asleep next to me. I remind myself that she isn't angry. Everything is fine. I kiss her quickly and climb over her. As I walk home, I text Mina. She's awake. An awesome thing about Mina is that she is always awake.

She answers the door in an old blue oxford of her dad's

that she's worn through at the elbows. It's misbuttoned. I follow her to the kitchen, and she paces around the big marbled island while I stand in front of her pantry, looking at the cereals. Mina's house is bigger and nicer than ours, but it looks like no one lives here. It's spare, and echoey, and freakishly clean. There's no entryway in my house. You just open the door straight into our crap, sneakers and backpacks, stacks of mail, the big bowl of keys. When you open Mina's door, there are two pillars, the same dark wood as the rest of the floors and banisters, with a panel of stained glass above them. When I was little, I wasn't sure if this meant Mina's house was fancy or haunted.

"What book were you reading?" I ask.

"What?"

"You have that look you get when you're in the middle of an intense part of a book."

"Oh." She stops pacing. "No, just thinking." She gets a bowl down for me and pulls the Honey Nut Cheerios out, which I do usually end up choosing.

"Thanks."

She sits down and takes a handful for herself.

"So, how are you feeling?"

"Hm?"

"About what happened last night?"

She looks at me all sharp. "What do you mean?"

"Your, you know, your moment? And what you told me? About Yale?"

"Oh, right."

"Did you sleep okay and everything?"

"Yes, of course. I've calmed down, totally." She stands up and leaves her handful of Cheerios right there on the table. She's pacing again.

"Come on," I say. "Talk to me. How are you?"

"I kissed Quinn?"

I freeze with my spoon halfway to my mouth. "You—what?"

"Yes, I kissed him." She goes back to her route around and around the kitchen table. "Like a martian with only the most rudimentary sense of how to act like a human teenager, completely out of nowhere, and then I just—I just ran inside? Like?"

"Hey, hey, hey." I make her sit down in her chair. I get her a glass of water. She's got her face in her hands and is making a sort of ongoing pained noise.

"This is the least of our problems!" I say.

"Yes, how true, thank you for the reminder," she says with her face still in her hands. "I cried in front of everyone and ruined Hollis's birthday when everyone was actually being sort of nice to me, and then when Quinn was also being nice to me, I went completely insane and attacked him. With my mouth. And now my life is over. I don't even have a life. I didn't know your life could end if you don't even have one, but apparently it can, because mine has."

"Why is your life over?"

"Were you not listening?" She slams her hands down on the table.

"Drink your water."

"Don't tell me what to do." She takes a sip.

"Well, Hollis isn't upset. I don't know how or why, but she's just not. And as for the others, you'd be surprised . . . no one really cares about anyone but themselves, especially now. No one will remember by Monday."

"Do you really believe that?"

"Yes," I say. "I really do."

"And Hollis said she wasn't angry? You're not ad-libbing?"

"What she actually said was, *Is she gonna be okay?*"

"Oh." Mina pushes the Cheerios around, packing them into a neat little mound. "Well, that's nice."

"And as for Quinn—"

She moans and covers her face again.

"Was it a bad kiss?"

"What?" She drops her hands. "Why would you ask that?"

"Just trying to figure out why you're upset about it. Did you not like it? I'll be honest. I was worried he'd try to kiss you and it would be awful because you were all upset. But it sounds like you kissed him?"

"Oh, I definitely kissed him. He was standing there minding his own business, and I kissed him."

"Did it not live up?" I have no idea how it works after something happens to you like what happened to Mina. How you get your firsts back when someone else took them from you. How you keep it from ruining those things forever. I guess you don't. I realize I'm stabbing my spoon into the bowl and making a mess.

"Um," she says, "no, no, I don't think it was bad. It was, uh, it was short?"

"I think it's hard for short kisses to be bad," I say.

"You were worried he was going to kiss me?"

"Yeah, I told you he liked you, didn't I?"

"Well," she says miserably, "he probably doesn't anymore. I acted so strange and like I hated him the entire time we walked home and then I randomly kissed him and then I sprinted away."

"Mina?" I sigh.

"What?"

"It sounds"—I slurp the rest of my honey milk—"like you did something kind of badass."

She takes the bowl from me. "Don't slurp." She gets up and leans against the sink, looking at me. "Stop laughing!"

"I'm not!" I say. I am. "I'm serious, it sounds like you rocked it. I mean, rough night, sure, but you still got some action. That's sick."

"I am going to kill you to death." But she's laughing now, too.

"And it's consequentless—"

"Not a word—"

"Cause it's Quinn. He never acknowledges that he's kissed someone after the fact. So he'll just go on acting normal. I bet you'll even still go to prom. He'll make some jokes, you'll make some jokes, we'll all dance, everything will be fine. No harm done. Nothing will change."

"Okay," she says. "Okay. Maybe you're right."

"Of course I'm right. And hey."

"What?"

"First-kiss vibes!" I raise my hand for a high five.

She stares at it. She stares at me. Then she shrieks, a sort of war cry, and throws herself at me, chasing me around and around the table.

"I'm sorry, I'm sorry—" I gasp, weak from laughing, holding my hands up in surrender and then grabbing both her wrists when she tries to smack me. "Come on, though. Was it?"

"Yeah," she grumbles, "kind of. Not counting, you know. Whatever." She fumes at me with her back against

the fridge and her wrists in my hands on either side of
her face.

"I'm sorry," I say again, "for real."

Her lips twitch. "It's fine. Just. Watch yourself."

"Or what," I say, "you'll beat me up?"

I mean it as a joke, but it comes out wrong. We're still
standing in that odd position, with me pinning her wrists.
Out of nowhere, I feel too hot. I can feel my heartbeat in
my face, in my temples. I drop her wrists.

"Are you okay?" she asks.

"Yeah." I turn away. "I'm tired. And hungover."

"Yeah, we need to go back to bed."

"I knew you didn't sleep," I say.

She rolls her eyes.

"Hey, can I sleep on the floor in the sleeping bag?"

"You're too big for it now," she points out.

"Am not!"

"And we're too old for sleepovers."

"It's not a sleepover if the sun's up," I say. "It's just a
nap. Come on, we can read *Harry Potter*."

"Okay," she says, her head cocked, considering me.
"But you're reading first. Otherwise, you'll fall asleep."
She turns to the stairs.

"You go up," I say. "I'll be right there. I'm gonna wash
my bowl."

"You're acting so strange," she says as she walks away.

I rinse out my bowl and set it to dry on the counter.
I clean up her little pile of Cheerios and refill the glass
of water to bring up to her. Then I go to stand in front
of the fridge. There aren't many cards up. One from my
family, and one from her cousins, a few others with much
younger kids. One picture of Mina as a toddler in small

red rain boots, squatting down to point at the pebbles on the shore of Lake Michigan, holding her dad's hand. Her Yale acceptance, printed out. And just below, there it is. They're on a hike—mom, dad, and three boys. The tallest has the youngest on his shoulders. He looks older than I am, but not by much. He's got a broad, good-looking face and is squinting into the sun. He's even wearing a Yale T-shirt. *Wishing you peace and joy in the New Year,* it says, *from Kate and Brian, Josh (16), Liam (17), and Daniel (21).* I take the card off the fridge and tear it into tiny pieces. I throw it in the trash, cover it with some paper towel. It doesn't feel like enough, though, so I take the whole trash out, replace the bag, and follow Mina upstairs.

12

Mina

I'm actually not, recent events notwithstanding, a fool. I am in fact very fucking smart. So I lie around the house all weekend gathering the facts and figures. Quinn has certainly been acting oddly. He's sort of been going out of his way to talk to me. He is always kind of looking at me lately. He probably had in fact mentioned me to Caplan. He offered to walk me home and didn't even try to shove me off his skateboard or physically kick me to the curb. But an urge to right the wrongs of childhood tormenting, to subvert that narrative, is not the same as a crush. And being curious what it would be like to put the freaky girl in a prom dress is a tale as old as time. Inherently wrong and grotesque, uncanny, and ultimately, illicit. Tempting. Like wanting to watch a pimple pop.

I tell all this to Caplan when we take a walk on Saturday, and he says he literally can't follow a single thing I've said, but if I'm comparing myself to a zit, I need

more psychiatric help than he in good faith can pro-
vide. Then he says I must be reading too many creepy
books and he's going to confiscate my copy of *Jane Eyre*.
I come this close to opening my mouth and admitting
I know Quinn may actually like me and asking what I
should do next, but I don't want to sound hopeful. It's
not that I'm embarrassed in front of Caplan. Somewhere in the country of childhood, between panic attacks and car sickness and the time he laughed so hard
he wet the bed, I lost the ability to be embarrassed in
front of him. But if I don't want to sound hopeful, it
must mean I don't want to feel hopeful, and hoping you
won't feel hopeful is basically the same thing as hoping.
On Sunday, he tries to get me to come with everyone to
swim at Little Bend. I say no chance. No more normal
all-American-girl fun for me.

That evening, my mom emerges from her room to
tell me my grandmother called, asking if we've sent the
full payment to Yale yet.

"I told her we had," she says, not looking at me.

"But we haven't?"

She is touching the molding on my doorframe gently
as if testing to see if it will crumble away.

"We haven't, right?" I say.

She sighs.

"Mom."

"We would have missed the deadline."

"You did it without talking to me."

"What is there to talk about?" She's already turned
to the side, like she's leaving, a slim shadow in the
hallway.

"I don't think I want to go to Yale," I say.

Finally, she looks at me. I wait for her to ask me why.

"They offered to pay for Yale," she says quietly.

"I got money from Michigan."

She doesn't move. She stands looking at the inside of my doorframe.

"I don't want to go to Yale. I'd rather stay home than go there."

"Please, Mina, don't become a rebellious teenager now. You've always wanted to go to Yale."

If one more person tells me that, I'll scream, I think as she turns to leave, but what I open my mouth and say is, "So it's about their money?"

"Excuse me?"

"Well, if I don't need their money, do you?"

She looks like I've slapped her. I try to feel bad, but I can't. I've gotten a reaction.

"It's about keeping a relationship with them. And a connection. To your past."

"You can just say to Dad."

"Mina." She puts a hand over her eyes as if we're not inside with all the lights turned off.

"It's not my fault we're not close to them," I say. "You can't send me to Yale to make up for it."

"I tried," she says, "with his friends, with those families. They all had kids your age."

My stomach folds in.

"They still invite us on that vacation. Every year. But when you said you never wanted to go again, I didn't ask why. I didn't complain. I know you haven't always found it easy to make friends—"

I step backward into my room and shut the door. I stand there, with something like nausea rising inside of me, pinching the inside of my arm to keep myself here. I wait to hear her walk away.

"I am not the only one who isolated us," she says to my door.

It is pouring on Monday morning, and the sky is so dark that I sleep through my alarm. I left my glasses in Hollis's bathroom, so I have to put in contacts, and for some reason, this minor inconvenience makes me so irritated that I ignore the mug of coffee my mom has left out for me, even though I know it's an apology.

Because of the rain, Caplan offers to drive, but he's running late after dropping off his mom. I can feel myself being cold in the car and wait for him to call it out, to talk and joke till I relent, but he's quiet, too. I walk into homeroom well after the bell like a miserable drowned rat. I can feel everyone looking at me, I assume because I'm late. But when I sit down and drop my bag onto my desk, I knock something to the floor. It's a tiny blue origami elephant.

Caplan's voice crackles to life over the loudspeaker. I put the small creature in my palm. I can feel people still looking and I think about putting it away in my bag, but don't want to crush it, so I put it back where it was originally placed, on the left corner of my desk, facing the board.

I find Caplan outside of the main office, still looking grumpy.

"So how cringey was that?" he asks.

"What?"

"My promposal?"

"What do you mean?" I'm trying to keep an eye on

the distant corner of the hallway. I don't want to be surprised by Quinn.

"I asked Hollis over the loudspeaker. Did you not hear?"

"No," I say. "Sorry, I was distracted." I hold out the blue elephant. "Am I being punked? Did you dare him to do this?"

"What's that?"

"An elephant."

"Yeah, I see that. Is it Quinn's?"

"I think so."

"Where'd you get it?"

"It was sitting on my desk when I walked in."

Caplan stares at the little elephant. Hollis walks up to us holding roses. She bops him on the head with them.

"Thanks for these. And I say yes, by the way."

Caplan is still a statue.

"What's up?" She follows his eyes down to my palm. "Who's this little guy?"

"Quinn put it on Mina's desk," he says finally.

"Oh my god." She shoves her roses into Caplan's arms and picks up the elephant. "That is so cute I could die." She hands it back to me. "Wait, so are you and Quinn going out now?"

"No, what?" My shirt feels too tight around my neck.

"It's just an elephant," Caplan says stupidly, clutching his roses.

Mercifully, the bell rings, and Hollis glides away, but not before telling me she hopes I'm feeling better. I tell her I am, thank you, never better, breathing through my nose and reminding myself that I know the closest routes to the single-stall bathrooms from any spot in the school by heart.

I plan to avoid lunch altogether since I'm beginning to accept that everyone has lost their minds and I don't understand anything or anyone anymore, but it's still raining, so we're all quarantined to the cafeteria. I confuse myself as I walk in, torn between my usual move to stare at my feet, and my anxiety to know where in the room Quinn is. I get stuck somewhere in the middle, looking straight ahead, beelining for a table in the corner that is empty except for Lorraine Daniels, her red glasses a beacon of safety. Because of this, I don't see Quinn until he steps directly in front of me.

"Hi!" he sort of shouts at me.

"Hey," I say.

"No glasses," he says, pointing like he's going to touch my face and then quickly folding his arms.

"Yes, I misplaced them."

"You look nice," he says.

"Oh," I say.

"Sorry." He scratches the side of his head. "I'm being super weird."

"That's okay—"

"I meant to text you like all weekend and then waited too long and made it a thing in my head and then couldn't do it and I thought maybe you'd be at Little Bend since you've been coming around more but then you weren't so instead I left you the elephant and I meant to just give it to you in the hallway but then you were late so I went to leave it at your homeroom desk but everyone watched me as I did it and I realized it was probably a weird thing to do but then it was too late so I just left it on your desk and dipped. I hope I didn't embarrass you or something."

I make myself shut my mouth. "That's okay," I say, raising my fist, which I've kept locked carefully around the elephant all morning, and open it for him like a flower. The elephant is lying there on his side. Quinn reaches out and rights him with careful fingers.

"You still like elephants, right? I remember you did that awesome report on them in, like, fourth grade and your diorama, like, put everyone else to shame. You said they were your favorite animal because they were lucky and wise and remembered everything."

"That's—that's right—they do," I hear myself say.

"Sick," he says.

"Okay, well."

"Do you wanna hang out this week?"

"What?"

"Like see a movie or something?"

"Like, a date?"

"Only if you want to," he says, uncrossing and then recrossing his arms. "Yeah, we don't have to. It's all good—"

"No, I want to," I say.

"Really?"

"Yes."

"Okay, awesome. I'll text you."

"Okay." I turn to leave.

"Wait, do you, like, want to come eat with us?"

"No thank you," I say quickly, feeling faint, "but please text me."

I force myself calmly through the cafeteria, with the vague idea of going to sit at the table with Lorraine, but I can't seem to be able to alter my path, so I head for the closest exit that leads outside. As I turn, I see Quinn in my periphery with his hands in his pockets, doing a funny little skip back to his table. Someone gives him a high five. I throw myself against the doors, out into the warm rain.

13

Caplan

"God, she's weird," Quinn says happily, watching Mina through the glass cafeteria windows, stomping off in the downpour.

"So she said yes?" Hollis asks.

"Yeah, I'm weak. I can't believe it. Thanks for making me. Caplan said there was no way."

"Why would you say that?" Hollis asks me.

I shake myself. I've been feeling strange all day. Bleary and numb, like sleepwalking. "I just didn't think Mina was the dating type. She's not even, like, the friend type."

"Yeah, remember when she literally didn't talk for like a year in middle school?" says one of the guys, Noah. Noah, who I'm pretty sure poured the vodka on Mina.

"All you morons could stand to talk less," Hollis says.

"I just think it's weird she doesn't have any friends who are girls," Becca says.

"Yeah, red flag," says Ruby, who literally always agrees with Becca.

"She doesn't have any friends, period, besides Cap," says another one of the boys.

Hollis nudges me with her elbow. I blink at her.

"She has other friends," I say.

"She has other loners she sits with," says Becca.

"Quinn," Hollis says, turning toward him, "I think it's awesome."

"Thanks, Holly," he says, but he's looking at me, not Hollis.

"Me, too," I say.

Regrettably, Becca walks with us to history.

"Ugh," she's saying to Hollis, "so we like her now?"

"Becca, we are hot girls, not mean girls," Hollis says. "And being bitter is for losers."

"I'm not bitter—"

"I know you wanted Quinn to take you to prom—"

"That is just—I never even said—" Becca splutters.

"But this is all for the best because Noah wants to ask you. He told Caplan so."

"Wait, really?"

Hollis gives me a hard poke in the back.

"Yes," I say.

"What exactly did he say?"

I tune out as Hollis takes over and they set to discussing Noah's height and whether or not Becca can still wear heels. I wonder if Hollis has already clued Noah in or if I am going to have to play some part.

As I sit down in history, I pull out the paper that Mina did end up editing for me late last night. Everything's annoying me today for no reason. I can't pretend that the idea of Quinn taking out Mina is a personal thrill. I've worked for the whole part of my life that I can remember, the whole part that counted after that brief spell in elementary school, to look out for her. To make sure she's safe and happy. And now I'm going to watch my second-closest friend take her for a test drive and then potentially hurt her feelings. Quinn's a flirt. He flirts with everyone and has endless flirting currency but no follow-through. I'll be involved. They'll drag me in. It'll be messy. Best-case scenario, it'll be awkward, and my big wish for Mina, whose whole life has been one terrible unfair thing after another, is to have some ease. Some fun. I just wanted to get her to prom. And don't even get me started on Hollis's support. Knowing her, there's something else afoot. I don't want anything afoot. I want everything to stay normal, and I'm also feeling sick of everything and everyone. The two feelings are a bad cocktail.

For the first time, I allow myself to consider that Mina really might also go to Michigan. That it might, in the end, be the best thing for her. That if everything is about to change—and end—the one thing that would just stay the same would be the two of us. The idea is a relief. How many times have I learned not to assume what is right for Mina? If she wants to go to Michigan, I shouldn't fight her on it. I'm not much of a fighter, anyway.

She rushes into class with the bell, head down and dripping wet, and sits in front of me. I kick the back of her chair. She flips me off without turning around. I kick her chair harder, and she turns, with a funny combination of blush and pride on her face.

"What?"

I beam at her. "Are you excited for your date?"

"Yes. Don't make fun of me or you'll ruin it."

"I would never."

"I know it's—but if everyone else is going to act insane, so will I," she says and then turns back to the board. I lean forward.

"I was thinking—"

"Please change the subject."

"I know. I was about to."

"Fine. What?"

"I know the reason you don't want to go to Yale couldn't be more fucked up or unfair, but I'm so excited you might go to Michigan."

She turns toward her shoulder, so I can see half her face, one dimple, so I know she's smiling.

"Really?" she says.

"Yeah. Let's just do whatever we want forever."

The next day, the sun comes out, and all of a sudden it's summer. The school's AC has been broken for as long as we can all remember, which means it's disgusting inside, but I never mind because it always means we're getting close to vacation and there's something fun in complaining about it all together, even the teachers. I lie on the floor in Spanish, because Mr. Ochoa is cool and doesn't give a shit as long as we do our work, and heat rises, obviously. Quinn says from above me where he's drawing a dick on the side of the desk, "I can't believe this is the last time we'll have sweaty balls in our sweaty high school."

"Do you think you've drawn enough dicks on enough desks?"

"Not even close," he says. "But an artist's work is never done."

"Let's watch *Superbad* tonight."

"I can't," he says, using his eraser to make some highlights. "I'm going to the movies with Mina."

"Oh shit, that's right. What are you seeing?"

"That movie about Blake Lively fighting a shark." He looks at me. "What?"

"Nothing," I laugh.

"Hey, she picked it," he says. "It was that or something called *Me Before You.*"

"Sounds romantic."

"Do you think it matters"—he frowns at his desk dick—"that she didn't pick the romantic one?"

"Hey, don't ask me," I say. "You're going where no man has gone before. There's no map for Mina."

This makes him grin. "I'm a man on the moon."

"No, you're still on the treasure hunt."

He turns the dick into a rocket ship and is just starting work on all the planets when Mr. Ochoa comes over and gives him detention, but not before cracking up.

For three years in a row, somewhere around elementary, I was an astronaut for Halloween and Quinn was a pirate. My mom has a picture of each consecutive year printed and framed in my room. We did it again this year for old times' sake. Hollis wanted to murder me, because she had this whole plan for us to be Daphne and Fred. I think we broke up over it, actually—more of a symptom than the cause—but we made up at the Halloween party. She still wore the purple dress and the green scarf thing, and I'm only human. We made a lot of jokes that night about the doghouse.

I text her—

> remember when we had sex in the bathroom on halloween and Quinn walked in by mistake and you called him a meddling kid and slammed the door

She responds right away—

> Yeah I do

Then—

> It's so fucking hot I want to die. I'm in a sports bra in the library

I say—

> dress code

She says back—

> Doghouse.

> woof

> I'm sweaty.

> gross

> Should we have sex in the library?

> yeah probably.

> Come here.

> actually?

> No, of course not.

Then—

Third floor girls room is out of order

coming

We're late to lunch, and no one's at the usual table outside, so we check the caf. I'm shocked to see Mina sitting with everyone. She has her book open in front of her, but she's there at the table next to Quinn. When we sit down, she's actually laughing.

"Why are we inside?" Hollis asks.

"Well, Mina sat in here, and I followed her," Quinn says. "But where were you guys, and why are you so sweaty?"

"Everyone's sweaty," Hollis says, pulling me down to the other side of the table. Everyone else is here, too. I guess they followed Quinn. "Get your mind out of the gutter."

"Can't," he calls. "I live there."

Mina snorts. He makes a face at her, scrunching up his nose. She makes one back.

"It's definitely weird," Hollis says to me in a low voice as some other conversation strikes up, and Mina looks back to her book, biting down on a little smile. "But I also think they make sense."

"I don't know about all that," I say, "but she seems happy."

"Yeah, Quinn is, too. They were texting till three a.m."

"How do you know that?"

"Quinn told me. He said he felt like a seventh grader, in a good way, giggling at his phone under the covers. He sent me screenshots."

"I didn't get screenshots—"

"Cause you're not good at texting."

I don't have an argument there, so I take the apple from in front of her and bite into it. It's warm mush.

"She's really funny," Hollis says, now considering Mina, who's back to reading but with that little smile on half her face. "I didn't realize she was so funny."

"I've been saying that to you for years," I say. "This apple is gross. Everything in here is warm and gross, including us. We're all sitting in a warm, gross pot getting hotter and hotter, and we're gonna boil alive and not notice."

"You haven't, actually," says Hollis, now considering me with the same look. "You've always said you wanted us to be friends, but you never really tried to make it happen."

"I would do anything," I say, "to not have this same conversation again."

"Fine. Wanna come over tonight since all your other friends are busy?"

"I have more friends . . ."

"Cap." She takes my face in her hands and gives me a little shake. "I'm teasing you. Stop being grumpy."

"Sorry," I say, pushing my forehead against hers for a second and then pulling away. "Yeah, I'll come over. I just have to help hype Mina up first."

"I should come, too," Hollis says. "What are you gonna suggest for her outfit? The classic black Cons? Basketball shorts and a striped T-shirt?"

"Hey, I didn't get screenshots," I say. "Let me have this."

"Fine," she says. "FaceTime me in if you need me."

Just then, Noah squeezes in between us.

"Yo, Hollis let slip that one of the girls recently said she was into me, but she won't say who because girl code or some shit." He rolls his eyes at Hollis. She takes a delicate bite of her salad, ignoring him. "But I need a date to prom, and sophomore Sophie turned me down." I laugh halfway through my sip of water and he claps me on the back. Hollis gets up at that moment to toss her trash. I'm still choking, and Noah says, "Can you find out for me?"

I clear my throat and beckon him closer. "I already know. It's Becca. But you didn't hear it from me."

"Good looks," he says and rejoins the other end of the table.

"You should get an A-plus for all your work on prom," I say to Hollis as she sits back down. "Your greatest project so far." More shit talking always goes on when we sit inside, because the indoor tables are long, like the Last Supper. The outdoor tables are round and intimate. Harder to get away with side plotting or mid-game commentary when everyone is facing each other. Obviously, this is something Hollis first pointed out to me.

"Thank you very much," she says. "The genius of this was not telling him outright, because boys are naturally curious, like toddlers, and they like to conquer small tasks and mysteries. Plus, once they have an intense thought about something, they can't even tell what kind of thought it is. The ball just rolls."

"All the way to prom."

"Exactly."

"Everyone should know who was responsible for manipulating them," I say. "They owe you a thank-you."

"I just want us all to be together. And it's important to do good deeds," she says seriously, "especially when no one's watching."

When I go over to Mina's that afternoon, I find her in her bedroom, lying face down on the bed, with all her clothes all over the floor.

"I have to cancel," she says, her voice muffled in the pillow.

"Okay," I say, stepping over the clothes. "How come?"

"Because everything I try on makes me look like I'm playing dress-up and I'm all sweaty and I would really rather just watch a movie with you."

This gives me a dumb little whoop of joy in my stomach.

"Yeah, no shit. That's always what we'd both rather do," I say, picking up some of the discarded dresses. "But life persists."

She flips over onto her back and glares at her ceiling fan.

"That's my app's word of the day. *Persist.*"

"That's a little easy for you, I think," she says.

I hold out the blue dress she wore to Hollis's birthday. "You should just wear this one again," I say. "It looked good."

"What do you mean, 'It looked good'?"

"I mean I looked at it, and to me, it looked good and not bad."

"Well, I can't do that, because then it looks like I only own one dress like fucking Cinderella."

"Cinderella is like the hottest princess."

"Cinderella was a loser pushover with no dad."

I can think of absolutely nothing to say to this. She passes me her phone.

"Make up an excuse and be believable but also kind." She rolls back over onto her stomach. "And then leave me here to die."

I open her messages with Quinn. He's texted her.

> im scared of sharks and dates but im also so excited to see you
>
> whats up with that?

"You have a text." I hand her the phone.

She looks at it. She makes this face for one second, a face I've literally never seen her make, with her mouth sort of open. Then she bites down on her lip and flops back onto the bed. "Mother fuck fuck fuck."

"All right." I stand and pull out my own phone. "Three fucks. Time for the big guns." I FaceTime Hollis.

"What are you doing?"

Hollis picks up with the smuggest look of all time. Upon hearing her voice, Mina's eyes go wide, and she starts shaking her head vigorously.

"Hi," I say to Hollis, swatting Mina away. "You were right and I was wrong and we need help." I duck as Mina throws a shoe at me. She's hissing something about this being a very vulnerable moment.

"Okay, let me talk to Mina."

I hold the phone out. Mina literally stomps her foot, and then takes it.

"Hi," she says to Hollis, totally composed. "Sorry, this is embarrassing—"

"Are you joking?" Hollis says. "This is my favorite thing. Do you want to look fuckable or adorable?"

"Um, I guess, like, both?"

"Totally," Hollis says. "Okay, do you have a plain white tank top, like the kind we wear in gym?"

"Yes?"

"Right, you're gonna put that on and have Caplan make a little cut on the side like right beneath your boobs. Or a little lower, whatever you feel good in. And then take it off and crop it to that length."

"Okay—"

"And do you remember that white skirt you wore in ninth grade for the spring chorus concert?"

"Um, yes, I think."

"I've been thinking about it lately. I want to wear one like it to my grad dinner, but I can't find the right thing anywhere, like simple, cotton, A-line, *Sisterhood of the Traveling Pants* Lena in Greece vibes—"

"It's from Old Navy, like ten years ago."

"Do you still have it?" Hollis asks.

"I might," Mina says. "I have to look. It'll be small on me now?"

"Just try it for me. Cap, go get scissors!"

When I come back into the room, Mina's on her hands and knees in the depths of her closet.

"Okay," she says to Hollis, "found it."

When she pulls out the skirt, a small, yellowed rectangle of paper flutters to my feet.

"Amazing. So wear the skirt and the tank top and then Caplan's dark-wash jean jacket. It's on the floor of his car, I think."

"What's this?" I ask Mina, picking up the bit of paper.

"Won't it be big on me?" Mina asks Hollis.

"That's the idea," Hollis says, "tiny skirt, tiny shirt, big jacket. But call me back if it looks shitty." She hangs up.

The paper I'm holding looks like something from a vintage scrapbook. "What's *Chrysanthemum*?" I ask her. "And who are all these people?"

Mina sighs. "It's nothing. It's garbage." She puts the skirt and the tank top on the bed.

I hold up the scissors.

She glares at them. "Should you just stab me?"

"Mina."

"Not, like, in the heart. Like in the thigh, or even the calf, just somewhere bad enough that we can go to the emergency room instead."

"Do you really not want to go?" I ask. "Cause you don't have to."

We look at each other for a moment.

"It's okay," I start to say. "You can tell me—"

"I really, really do want to go," she says suddenly.

"Well. Okay, then. Let's crop a top."

"Close your eyes."

She turns around and starts to pull her T-shirt over her head. I shut my eyes. Out of nowhere, I feel awkward. Like, intensely awkward. Like if I don't say something, the room is going to explode, or like I'm going to lose control of my body and open my eyes by accident and then what would I even see but Mina's back and there is nothing sexy about a back so it wouldn't even matter and I don't know why I'm thinking about it at all, maybe just because I'm adjusting to the idea of a Mina who wants to go on dates. And look fuckable.

"I'm just gonna go get that jacket," I say very loudly.
I try to leave with my eyes closed and walk into the wall.

I stomp across the street, and the jacket is just where
Hollis said it would be.

I offer to drive Mina to the movie theater, but she tells me
I'm not dropping her off on a date like I'm her father's
ghost. Then I wander around my house from room to
room until my mom tells me to leave because I'm stress-
ing her out, so I walk to Hollis's.

"Did Mina just get in a car with Quinn?" Oliver asks,
passing me on his way inside.

"Yeah."

"God, you're dumb."

"What's that supposed to mean?"

He just shakes his head.

"Go jerk off," I say.

"You go jerk off."

"I don't need to. I'm going to see my girlfriend. That's
like a special person who is a girl and your friend, but
when you're alone together—"

He leans back out the door and hurls his lacrosse
stick at my head, but it misses.

On my way to Hollis's, I take the bit of paper from
Mina's floor that she'd called *garbage* from my pocket. I
mean to toss it in one of the bins that have been brought
out, since it's trash day tomorrow, but then I realize what
it is. Mina used to have a collection of them when we
were little—these cards from old libraries. I get stuck
looking at the list of names. On a faded inked chart it
says Eleanor Jacobs, August 16, 1996. April Halloway,

September 1, 1996. Maggie Briggs, September 14, 1996. Then Eleanor again, like six times in a row. And then, at the very bottom, Kitty Jacobs, June 11, 1997. I flip the card over. In handwriting that is like Mina's, but smaller and softer, it says "*Chrysanthemum* by Kevin Henkes, Mina's first favorite book, 2001." I put the card, careful not to fold or crease it, back into my pocket.

"How'd she look?" Hollis asks me once I've collapsed onto her bed.

"Like you," I say.

"That's not even true. I really tried to be thoughtful of her style and how to elevate it without imposing my own—"

"I'm kidding. She didn't look like you, but she did look nice."

"You don't look like you're kidding," she says.

"How do I look?"

"I don't know."

She lies down next to me and starts drawing with her fingers on my arm.

"Can I just ask," I start carefully, "why are you so into this?"

"Isn't it obvious?"

"No," I say, "nothing anyone is doing right now is obvious to me."

"Well," she says, "it might be kind of a relief to not feel like you have two girlfriends anymore."

This stuns me. "Is that how you feel?"

"Not really. I'm being dramatic."

I say nothing.

"All right, yeah, sometimes. Like Mina's your emotional girlfriend and I'm you're—I don't know. Sex girlfriend."

"Jesus—that's terrible." I laugh. "Don't say that about yourself."

"It's fine," she says. "It's my fault, too. If I were a less jealous person, I wouldn't care that your best friend is a girl, and then we'd have no problems."

Hollis's self-awareness flows like this, so easily. I'm busy being impressed and jealous so I almost miss what she says next.

"I was also just sure she was secretly in love with you."

"She's definitely not."

"She definitely was," she says, "but I don't think she is anymore." Her hands go still on my arm, and I realize she's waiting for me to talk.

"Whatever you say."

"I think," she says, "it all might feel a little more balanced now."

"Well, good, then."

"I used to wish you and I were the kind of couple that called each other *best friends*."

"Those couples are a snooze," I say, "and probably never fuck."

"So true."

"Wanna take a shower?"

She laughs, rolling away from me.

"Come on, sex girlfriend." I yank her toward me and put her over my shoulder.

"That's so not funny."

"Then why are you laughing so much?"

.   .   .

Then, in the shower, I can't get hard. This isn't shocking or unheard of. It just hasn't happened to me in a while. Actually, it probably hasn't happened since sophomore year. I feel fifteen again. I really want her to stop looking at my face. I try to think of something funny to say about it.

"I'm sorry," I say.

"I don't care at all," she says, sitting on the edge of a tub in her towel. "I only care when you get all weird and upset about it."

"Okay, well, I'm not acting weird."

"But do you feel weird?"

"I feel incredibly normal."

"'Incredibly normal.' Okay." She looks at me for a second. Then she gets up and puts her arms around me.

"I'm sorry," I say again.

"It's really fine."

"Want me to finger you or something?"

"No, that's okay. Wanna brush my hair?"

"Sure. Or, well, it's kinda late. I should go home."

"All right."

She goes to the mirror and looks at herself, twisting all her hair over one shoulder and wringing it out into the sink.

I let myself out.

On my walk home, I text Mina and ask her how it's going. She doesn't reply, which I take to mean that it is all fine and she isn't hiding in the bathroom or anything. I check her bedroom window when I get back, but it's dark. Then, just as I'm heading up my driveway, Quinn's car comes around the corner. To be clear, Quinn doesn't have a car, but his older brother who goes to State does. He never lets Quinn borrow it unless Quinn makes him a very good deal, and even then Quinn has to take the bus to East Lansing to get it. The last time we wanted his car for something, Quinn had to DD for his brother's whole fraternity for three weekends in a row.

I pause in my driveway, waiting for them to see me as they get out so I can wave. I think maybe I'll ask Quinn if he wants to smoke, but they walk to her front door without noticing me. Mina has her arms locked behind her back, gripping both her elbows. Suddenly, I feel weird as fuck just standing there watching them, but I also don't want them to hear me opening my door, so I sort of turn and shuffle and blink, and then they are making out. Like really fucking making out, hanging on to each other and swaying on the spot. I panic and duck down behind the trash cans at the end of the driveway. I squat there like a freak, hanging on to my knees and breathing like I've just run miles. Like someone's dropped something really heavy on my head. Like the whole sky. I look up at it. It feels like the street is swinging up to meet the stars. I think vaguely of how bad it would be to be caught in this position, crouching behind the trash. I decide it makes the most sense to crawl up my driveway on my hands and knees so they won't see me, but as soon as I start doing that, I feel very fucking silly, so I force myself to be normal. Feel normal, act normal, just stand up and whistle at them or something, but when I do stand, I see that Quinn has his hands on her ass. The white skirt is up around her waist. She's wearing plain white underwear.

I make myself turn around and walk up my driveway. I keep myself from running or slamming the door. In the event of an emergency, proceed calmly toward the exits, and all that. My mom tries to talk to me as I pass her on the stairs, but something is wrong with my ears, so I just go to my room and lie the wrong way on the bed and stare at the ceiling.

Hollis once said to me that boys are so stupid about their own feelings, they don't realize they have a problem until it's a tumor. I decide, around four in the morning, that I will not let that happen to me. I will not be stupid. I will not be in denial. I will get ahead of this.

I am attracted to Mina. That is fine. This day was, I guess, always going to come. People are friends with people they're attracted to. It happens every day. People are friends with hot people without it ruining their lives. I am probably only feeling this way because she is now attracted to someone else, my good friend, and that is human nature. This is very natural, no big deal, and I am on top of it.

The next day at school, I walk out of first period and she's standing with Quinn at the water fountain. When she bends over to take a drink, he puts his hands on her waist and bangs her hips into his. She laughs so hard she does a spit take. While I'm looking at them, I walk directly into an open classroom door and smack my head so hard I see stars.

It occurs to me that I might already have a tumor.

14

Mina

After the first and only date I've ever been on, I shut the door and sit on the floor. I put my head in between my knees. I tell myself—this, whatever it is I'm feeling, is not bad.

I repeat it to myself, holding my shins. This feeling is not bad. I realize I am smiling. I am on the edge of a laugh, but I can't remember what was funny. Only that we were sort of laughing and sort of kissing. This feeling is not bad.

Of course in great works of film and literature, kissing is like fireworks. I don't feel any fireworks. Then I remember, as a child, I used to sob every year on the Fourth of July because they were too big, too bright, and too loud. So this is all for the best.

I close my eyes again and send my brain all around my body. Everything seems in order. I don't even have a stomachache even though I ate a hundred Twizzlers.

When I go upstairs, my mom's light is on, spilling out into the hallway. I peer in, but she's asleep. I go to turn off her lamp.

"I tried to stay awake," she mumbles. "I wanted to hear about your date."

"It's okay. Go back to sleep, Mom."

"I know you said it wasn't a real one . . ." She sighs and tucks her hands under her cheek.

"I think it was, actually. A real one."

"A real date?"

"Yes."

She smiles without opening her eyes. I wait for her to say something, but she's fallen back asleep. I go to the bathroom to wash my face and brush my teeth but get stuck looking at myself in the mirror, trying to decide if I look any different. My lips are swollen and my face is flushed. I feel split open. I feel embarrassed, but I also feel pretty. My mouth looks different. Maybe it just feels different, I don't know.

Then I get under the covers without doing any of my nighttime routine. I have texts from Caplan asking how it all went. I tell him I'm sorry for my behavior earlier and thank him for calming me down. I tell him it was really fun and that maybe I'm going to grow up to be a normal person, after all.

The next day, I feel like I am walking around inside of someone else's life. Quinn walks with me between classes, so close that our shoulders are touching.

"People are staring," I say to him.

He tries to hold my hand, and I push him into a trash can. I don't even really have time to mind that people are looking at me, because I can't stop laughing.

We arrive at history, and I realize he has walked me to class. He pauses in the doorway, in full view of everyone at their desks. Our teacher isn't there yet. They watch us like a movie.

"This is sort of crazy," I say, wishing I'd worn my hair down and only he could see my face.

"Not in a bad way, though, right?" he asks.

"I don't really know yet."

"Well, you let me know." He takes a deep breath like he's hyping himself up, shoves his hands down into his pockets.

"What?"

"I was gonna kiss you on the cheek or something."

"Don't do that. I'll die of embarrassment."

He gets a glint in his eye and does it, so fast he bangs his chin into mine, and then literally runs away.

"Hi!" Caplan shouts at me as I sit down in front of him. He's leaning so far forward that both back legs of his chair are up.

"Calm down," I whisper.

He drags his chair up between my desk and the one on my right. It's Lorraine Daniels's, and she is, blessedly, sketching in a notebook and completely ignoring us.

"So, give me all the gossip."

"There isn't any gossip. I told you, it was really nice."

"Are you going steady?" He scoots his chair closer to me.

"Stop it."

"Ms. Cane isn't even here."

"You're being a show-off."

"What, and you're not?"

A substitute walks in, dragging an ancient TV on wheels. She kills the lights, and something clicks off inside of me. I look straight ahead and try not to cry. It's one thing to feel like I'm pretending to be someone else. To feel foolish. It's another thing to look it.

"Mina," Caplan whispers. I shake my head. "Mina, I'm sorry, I was just kidding."

We sit there in the dark, watching a documentary about the bubonic plague. I can feel Caplan looking at me the entire time. Eventually, I can't stand it, so I ask to go to the bathroom. I know immediately he's going to follow me.

"Caplan, drop it."

"Mrs. What's Her Face says we need to walk together cause there's only one hall pass."

"How convenient."

When I finally look at him, his eyes are wide, and he's chewed his bottom lip to shreds. There are dark purple moons under his eyes.

"What's going on with you?" I ask.

"Oh, you know, the Black Death doesn't really do it for me."

I laugh by mistake.

"You're not showing off. Quinn is. And he should, because you're—you know—yeah. I'm sorry. It was a stupid thing to say."

"It's all right," I say. "It is kind of weird. It's totally weird."

"It's not."

I roll my eyes.

"Stop it. It's not. Can I hug you?"

This is something else, left over from when we were younger. For years, I would jump if anyone touched me. Caplan would always ask. As I got better, I told him he didn't need to anymore, but he does it still, every now and then. I never know if it's an accident, or an instinct, or something in between.

"Sure," I say.

"Friends again?" he asks, holding on to me for longer than I expect him to.

"Just don't be a dick," I say.

"Got it. Can do."

We break apart and walk back to class.

"Didn't you have to pee?" he asks.

"Didn't you?"

"No," he says, smiling, "not really."

"Me neither."

At lunch, I feel nervous that Quinn will act like my boyfriend and it will be awkward, but he can't really, because everybody talks to me. I do sit next to him, and if I ever can't think of what to say, he jumps in. People who have never spoken to me before call my name across the table. I think that people are noticing me and being nice to me just because of Quinn, because of a boy, and that's how high school works. I type this out in a note and hand my phone to Caplan. He types back that maybe it's actually because I put my book away today.

I shake myself as Ruby says my name for the second time.

"Wanna come, Mina?"

"Sorry, I spaced out."

And then she smiles at me, like I've done something classic and endearing. Like she knows me. "We're gonna pre at my house tonight," she says. "Are you coming?"

"Oh." I look at Quinn, sure that if he'd wanted me

there, he'd have told me about it. This is the strategy I employ with Caplan. I used to not even go on field trips unless he specifically asked me to, in case he wasn't in the mood to babysit me. But Quinn doesn't tell me what to do. He's just smiling at me.

"Sure, yes, that sounds fun," I say to Ruby. "Thank you."

"How sick is it Mina's coming out?" Quinn says to Caplan, with an arm loose around my shoulders as we leave lunch.

"Yeah, it's great! It's so great."

"What's the pregame for?" I ask.

"Oh, some house party a St. Mary's kid is throwing."

"Are you sure I'm invited?"

Quinn laughs like I've said something cute, so I look at Caplan, but he says nothing. He's looking at our sneakers. When we get to French, I realize they've both walked me to class.

"Caplan, wait a sec?"

Quinn tugs on my ponytail and lopes off down the hallway.

"Is this okay?" I ask.

Caplan blinks. He opens his mouth and closes it and opens it again. We talk at the same time.

"What, you and Quinn?"

"The party tonight?"

He stares at me.

"I don't have to go," I say. "To the party or the pregame, I mean, this is your life and your friends, and I don't need to—"

"What are you talking about?"

"You were so quiet during lunch—"

"Mina, this is all I've wanted, for you to be around. I ask you every single Friday to come out with us."

"So this is all okay with you?"

He looks at me with this strange face, biting down on his lip again, nothing like himself. I'm about to say that I actually don't want to go, if it's such a thing—

"Yeah. Yeah, it's more than okay."

Then the bell rings, and I watch him jog off down the hallway, just to be stopped at the corner and given a late slip.

In French, I have my computer open because we're playing some sort of online trivia. Out of nowhere, I have a million iMessages, dinging and dinging. Madame glares at me, and I quickly mute my computer. A number I don't recognize has added me to a group chat of numbers I also don't recognize.

I have never been in a group chat that wasn't for a school project before.

YAYyyy Mina!!! someone says with the firework emoji. Something very intense happens in me, not unlike a firework. A silent symphony of shock and awe.

Everyone say names, says the number who added me. Everyone does. It becomes clear the first number is Hollis. My hands are shaking and I type and delete and type and delete, and eventually land on the seminal classic— OMG hi!

The group chat is called NO BONERS. I spend the rest of French watching a play unfold on my laptop:

What are we wearing

when are we leaving

Noah just burped in class

My stomach hurts I'm being so brave

I'm waiting in the bathroom to take nudes but these
bitches wont leave I hate this place

I love it here is Mr. Ochoa hot or am I just really hungry

He's daddy and you're hungry

can we skip 8th and get food

no lets go after school

who has cars

lets go to Quickstop I want a hotdog

disgusting

that sounds so amazing you're a genius

Mina will you come!

We're definitely overwhelming her.

You're not! Yes to quickstop!

WOOOO

Do we have enough cars?

We'll squeeze

After school, I report to the side door where I always meet Caplan, but he texts me that it was his fifth tardy, so he has detention. I'm standing off to the side looking at my phone when the door bursts open, and they all spill out into the afternoon sun. Quinn tries to take my arm, but Hollis loops hers through mine and pulls me off with the girls.

"No fair!" Quinn calls out.

"Meet us there!" Hollis says.

I end up in Hollis's car, and she gives me shotgun.

"The trunk is the rite of passage," Becca says, her voice muffled as we pull off down the street.

"We're not hazing her!"

"Thank god," I say.

"Well," Hollis says.

She reaches across me and opens the glove compartment. There's a Smirnoff Ice inside. Everyone cheers for me as I take it.

"Do I have to chug it?" I ask.

"If I chug bubbles, I throw up immediately," says Ruby.

"You don't have to drink it at all," Hollis says. "It's ceremonial."

I crack it and take a sip. It isn't bad. Fake sugar, a tiny bite of alcohol, but nothing I recognize. Everyone is barely in their seats talking over each other about the thousand tiny triumphs and failures of the day, and hopes and dreams for the night. I spill a little bit on myself. My stomach tightens, and then I realize it'll just dry, and the thought makes me want to laugh out loud and roll the windows down, so I do. Hollis is a good driver, carving neatly through the mass exodus of kids leaving the school on foot. She tells me to pick a song, handing me her phone, and I briefly panic before realizing she has about a thousand playlists. I shuffle one called Girls Getting Ready. "Roses" by the Chainsmokers plays, which is a song I thought I hated. She turns the volume up so loud I feel the bass in my feet and my throat, something like happiness vibrating in my bones.

On the corner of the middle school, Hollis slows down and pulls up in front of a gangly freckled girl holding a gym bag. She peers into the car at all of us.

"So I'm walking home?"

"I'm sorry, Kel. I'll make it up to you—"

"Here," I say, opening the door. "We can squeeze."

She doesn't miss a beat, swinging her bag down at my feet and sitting right on my lap. She rebuckles the seat belt around us both.

"If you get me a ticket—" Hollis is saying.

"You've got two girls in the trunk! It's for two minutes!" Kelly says.

"Fine. Just slouch if you see a police car." I put my arms around this girl who I assume is Hollis's sister, because there's nowhere else to put them, but she seems perfectly comfortable with this and chats with me for the next few minutes. Her weight is foreign, but not bad.

"So, do you have sisters?"

"No," I say.

"Lucky you," she sighs. "I love your shoes." She looks down at my Converse. "So, who are you?"

"Kelly!" Hollis says.

"What? Sorry!"

"That's fine," I say. "I'm Mina."

"Nice to meet you, Mina. Thanks for letting me squeeze."

"Of course. I'm learning it's kind of your sister's policy."

"Yeah, when she's in the mood to feel like she's being nice—"

"Okay, for that, you can walk the last block," Hollis says.

Kelly rolls her eyes and jumps out.

The boys pull into the parking lot as we're getting out of the car. Quinn is hanging on to the side of Noah's Jeep. He swings off and lands on the ground like Spider-Man as they slide into a spot. On our way into

Quickstop, I see Lorraine Daniels sitting on the low wall out front with kids I don't recognize. I'm feeling giddy and a little manic with all my newfound social energy, so I wave at her. She looks surprised, and then Quinn drags me away.

Inside, he takes forever, sitting cross-legged in front of all the chips. He slanders each flavor: barbecue is for sluts, plain Lay's is for virgins, obviously, Cheetos are for nose-pickers, Fritos are for people who clap when planes land.

"Come on!" Hollis calls from the checkout line, waving at me from over the aisles. Quinn reaches from the ground and plays with the bottom of my skirt. Suddenly, I feel like we're alone. His fingertips pause, so light, above my knee. I force myself not to look away first.

"GUYS!" Hollis calls again.

Quinn rises up then, without uncrossing his ankles, all joints, still fluid, and grabs the big bag of Lay's.

"I'm going to say hi to my friend outside," I say as he joins the congestion at the register.

Lorraine doesn't look up until I'm standing right in front of her.

"Hi," I say.

She's smoking a cigarette. "Hey." She holds it out to me.

"No thanks," I say.

"Good for you, I guess," she says.

"Oh. No, no judgment, I've just never smoked before."

"I meant your ascent."

I blink at her.

"You got everything you ever wanted."

"Sorry?"

"You're breeding with that one now, right?"

Quinn bursts from the store, swinging his chips and a six-pack with obvious pride.

I stare at Lorraine. "I just wanted to say hi."

"Right." She turns to the boy to her left, who's been staring at the blinking neon sign for the duration of our conversation with his mouth hanging open, and asks him for another cigarette. Someone honks for me.

"His name's Quinn," I say, talking to her shoes.

"I know."

"So why'd you pretend not to?"

I turn and leave before she answers me, feeling dramatic and sort of embarrassed. I sit in the boys' Jeep with Quinn, the world roaring past all around us as we fly down the street, the afternoon sun turning everything slanted and gold. We go over a speed bump too quickly, and one of the boys standing in the back tips his chocolate milkshake all over me by mistake. This is the mess of other people, I think, all banging around too close together. Something always spills. But I lick some off my finger, and it's delicious.

When we get to Ruby's, she and Hollis rush me upstairs and strip me out of my white-and-chocolate shirt. I sit down on the bed and cross my arms over my stomach, but then Ruby comes over to me with a damp washcloth and starts to dab at the milkshake on my neck and collarbones. The gesture is so gentle and the expression on her face so sweet and focused that my arms unfold on their own. Hollis is combing through the dresses in Ruby's closet.

"Don't go wild, please," I say. Someone downstairs is yelling that they can't get the liquor cabinet unlocked, so Ruby goes, and Hollis turns around with a tiny piece of pale blue fabric.

"Very funny," I say.

"I'm not joking."

"If I walk down in that, everyone is going to laugh at me."

Hollis raises her eyebrows.

"What?" I say.

"You are the stupidest genius I ever met."

I suddenly feel miserable and homesick, not a ten-minute walk from my own bedroom. But I'm naked and sticky and completely at the mercy of the most terrifying person I've ever met and Caplan is god knows where and Quinn is downstairs probably expecting me to drink more and sit on his lap again and all I want to do is go home, but I can't stand up, because I'm not wearing a shirt and these two things are connected for some reason. Also if I make any sudden movements, I may cry.

"Oh god, don't make that face," Hollis says. "Look, just put it on, and if you look in the mirror and hate it, obviously I won't force you to wear it downstairs. No one will ever see it, not even me. I'll shut my eyes."

"But I know I'll hate it."

"Then why are you scared to try it on?"

I take the dress and turn away from her.

"So what was that girl's problem? Outside of Quick-stop."

"You heard her?" I ask, messing with the straps.

"It's a halter, just step into it. No, but she rolled her eyes at you like four times."

"She's a school friend. Or, I guess not really, just a person from school. She was making fun of me for hanging out with you guys."

I think I say it to be mean, because I'm angry and humiliated that she's playing dress-up with me.

Hollis just snorts. "Revenge of the nerds," she says. Then: "I'm sorry, that's such bullshit of her. That's like— like social slut-shaming. People only shit on you if you've offended them or if they're jealous of you, that's it. And did you ever offend her?"

"Not that I can think of," I say.

"Exactly. So don't let her ruin your fun."

"If that's true, then why were you always shitty to me?"

I hold very still, appalled with myself. Can I be drunk from one drink or one drop of attention? She puts her hands on my shoulders, and I flinch. She turns me around so I can see myself in the mirror.

"Come on, Mina. Why do you think?"

15
Caplan

When I finally get out of detention, I don't even bother going home to drop off any of my things or get the car. I walk straight to Ruby's and end up jogging the last few blocks with my backpack bouncing around stupidly. I'm convinced that if I leave Mina alone in Hollis's company, she'll arrange a wedding for her and Quinn faster than either of them can say, "I guess I do." The jog is a mistake, because when I get there I'm all sweaty and suffering from another feeling that I can't quite place.

At Ruby's, everyone is in her living room crowding around three flattened pizza boxes taped together and covered in Sharpie writing, names and dares, and my heart kicks into high gear. The last thing this fever dream needs is *Remove one article of clothing*. I don't see Mina or Hollis anywhere, and I'm about to go hunt for them when Quinn sees me. He calls out. Everyone looks up, and then I'm shotgunning a beer with my stupid backpack still on.

I'm on beer three when Quinn wolf whistles. I look up, and Hollis is coming down the stairs with a person I've never seen in my life, much less a person I've spent most of my life so far with. She's wearing a light blue dress with no back, and her hair is on top of her head and all kinda coming down around her face. She looks at me and sort of shrugs, her shoulders moving the blue dress up and down, and then she meets Quinn at the bottom of the stairs. He reaches out to her, and I close my eyes.

"Why's your backpack on?"

"Oh?"

Hollis takes it from me.

"Okay, yeah, thanks."

"Don't worry about her," Hollis says, following my eyes. "She's okay, really. She actually seems like she's having fun."

Mina is still talking to Quinn. Her arms are hanging loose at her sides with her palms open to him.

"Look at her posture. She looks like a whole different person. The power of a good dress."

"Oh," I say. "Yeah, I don't think guys really notice stuff like that."

I walk into the kitchen, which is mercifully empty. I run the tap till it's cold and then put my wrist under the water. This is something Mina once taught me. It's supposed to help with panic and nausea. I realize I hope I'm sick. I hope I'm coming down with the flu and this would all be explained away. Actually, I hope something is seriously medically wrong with me and I have to go to the hospital, because then I wouldn't have to figure

out what the hell I'm supposed to do next. I switch my
wrists.

"Hey!"

I jump and turn and Mina is there, gliding toward me
looking like a fucking figure skater.

"The water's running?"

"Right, yeah!" I switch it off and dry my hands on my
shorts.

Up close, she looks more like herself and also less.
She has freckles again and chapped lips, but her eyes are
bright and her cheeks are pink.

"So, are you having fun?" I ask.

"You know, I actually am." She starts to pace around
the kitchen. "This is going to sound pathetic because
we're just in high school and none of these feelings even
matter and this couldn't be any more trite—"

"You know, it's not actually your fault that you're in
high school. You can still, like, be in the moment sometimes. What's *trite* mean again?"

"Yes, that's exactly it! That's how I feel. I feel in the
moment, actually, for the first time in, I don't even know.
It's like—I've been so careful to keep myself held together,
and I've wound that mess so tight, and I was always sure
that if I took a deep breath it would all explode. But it's
like he pulled a loose thread or something and now it's
all coming apart but nothing is exploding, I'm just . . ."
She puts both her hands over her heart, then looks down,
surprised to find them there, and throws her arms up
in the air. When they float back down, she is smiling at
nothing. "I'm just breathing."

"Well," I say, "that's really awesome. Breathing is good,
right?"

"Right. And *trite* means, like, 'unimportant and un-original.'"

"Well. You're the opposite of trite. And so are all the things you do and say. And feel."

"Why are you looking at me like that?" she asks. "Do I look stupid?" She goes to fold her arms across her chest.

"No, no, don't do that again," I snap, pulling her arms back to her sides. She leaves them hanging, but links her pointer fingers in front of herself.

"You're still doing it."

"Am not," I say.

Suddenly, her mouth falls open. "Are you really being such a boy?"

"Huh?"

"Are you just staring like that cause you can, like, see my arms?"

I can't think of anything to say. She laughs, and I try to figure out how to rein in the conversation. Pull things back onto a plane that I understand.

"I'm disappointed in you," she says. "A little arm skin, that's all it takes?"

"Well," I say, reaching out and pushing the dish towel back and forth on its rod for something to do, "I do think your arms look nice. Is that so bad?"

"Nice?"

"Yeah, like, strong?"

"Oh my god—"

"Well, I'm sorry, but that was a real Hermione-on-the-steps-at-the-ball moment you just had. And don't act like it wasn't!" I sort of yell at her.

"God, I hate that scene."

"Really? I didn't know that."

"I mean, it's iconic, obviously," she says, taking the dish towel from me and folding it neatly again, "but they do that weird thing in the movie where Harry gazes at her. Harry in the book would never look at Hermione that way. It's totally Hollywoodified, and it devalues the simplicity and the strength of their friendship."

"What?" I say. "Can't it be both?"

"What do you mean?"

"Like he can't be her best friend and also look at her and realize she's, like, super beautiful?"

"Yeah, I mean, sure. Hey, are you okay?"

I rub my hands across my face. "Yes," I say. "Yeah, I just—I think I have a fever or something."

"A fever?" She tries to touch my forehead, and I jerk away.

"Yeah, or brain damage—"

"Caplan?"

"And I kinda miss you? Not in a weird way."

"Oh." Her face turns soft. "I miss you, too," she says.

"EVERYONE IN THE LIVING ROOM NOW!" Hollis yells from a universe away.

"Do you think," I say, "that we could walk home later, just us?"

"Of course, but are you sure—"

"Yeah, I'm totally fine, I just want to—uh, yeah, I just want to talk about some stuff?"

"What stuff?"

"Not important stuff—"

"If it's not important, then tell me now?"

"GUYS!" Hollis yells from the doorway.

Quinn ducks under her arm. "The master of ceremonies is impatient," he says.

Hollis elbows him in the stomach and beckons us again.

I can feel Mina looking at me, but I follow after Hollis and Quinn without another word.

We sit in a loose circle around the pizza boxes. There is a lot of pageantry around Mina adding her name in what little space is next, cramped by mine. I worry the whole thing is a little culty and condescending, but she doesn't seem to mind. Then Hollis takes the Sharpie and draws a larger circle around Mina's name and my name.

"So every time the quarter lands on Mina, Cap has to drink, too."

There is a roar of approval.

"You don't have to drink if you don't want to," I say to Mina quietly, but she isn't really listening.

Ruby goes first, and her quarter lands on *Give someone a lap dance*. She chooses Mina, of course, who covers her eyes, but is also giggling, in a very un-Mina-ish way.

Once in eighth-grade gym, we had to learn square dancing. It was a nightmare for everyone, paired off against our will and promenading around with our arms linked. I remember Mina was paired with Jim Ferraby, who was super quiet, also a nerd, and very nonthreatening. But when he tried to touch her elbow to do-si-do, she turned so pale she looked gray and broke out in a sweat. Five minutes later, she asked to go to the bathroom. She walked purposefully to the door with a straight face and neat little steps, but in the final moments before she cleared the threshold, I saw her getting ready to run. Mina was excused from gym after that with a note about anxiety. I remember the other girls saying it was because she looked so weird in the shorts. I don't remember whether that ever got back to her. I also don't remember if I defended her.

Ruby has her sweater off and is draping it around Mina's neck as she leans backward. Mina reaches out to steady her with a hand on Ruby's back. When Ruby sits up, they're nose to nose and both laughing too hard to keep going.

Then we waterfall, everyone chugging their drink in a cascade. Some of my beer drips under my chin. When it's Quinn's turn, he cheats and places his quarter right on Mina's name. Everyone thinks this is adorable. Before we both drink, she touches her seltzer to my beer in a cheers. She meets my eyes and then looks back at the game like it's nothing.

Noah has to watch porn with headphones on and narrate the whole thing out loud. Becca gets *Text or shot* and texts her SAT tutor: whats up daddy. Then she also takes the shot, for fun, I guess. Hollis loses her shirt. Then it's Mina's turn, and we play a sickening game of spin the bottle. I get that feeling again, like something huge is trying to get out of my chest, as the empty wine bottle goes around and around. I realize I can't tell if I would rather watch her kiss Quinn or have to kiss her myself, and then the bottle lands decisively on Jamie, who has no personality and no stake in whatever weird extended stroke I'm having. He is probably the least relevant person here. Good for him. I remind myself this is not a movie. This is just my life and a normal Friday night and a drinking game and the stakes are actually very low.

Mina raises her eyebrows at Quinn, and he salutes

her. Quinn has always been a good sport. She crawls across the circle on her hands and knees and pecks Jamie Whatshisname so quickly I miss it. They high-five after like they are old friends. The feeling in my chest has gotten worse, and I feel like the only thing to do to make it better would be to grab Mina's hand and drag her outside and down the street and far away and cry to her and tell her everything I feel, as if she has nothing to do with it all, like everything is back to normal, like it's a fight with Hollis or a shitty test grade or a call to my dad sent straight to voicemail, and she would make it all fine, somehow, just with the faces she would make and the things she would say to me.

"Caplan?"

I look at Hollis.

"It's your turn," she says. She looks annoyed.

I can't think what I could have possibly done this time, since I haven't said anything to her all night. Then something clunks into place, and I realize that is probably exactly what I've done. I try to smile at her, but my face isn't working. I flip the quarter high without looking at the board. It lands on *JJ*, with a big star around it.

"JACKIE JENESSEN RULES!"

"WOOOOO!"

Quinn drumrolls on the carpet, and even Hollis claps her hands together, forgetting her bad mood.

"What's *JJ*?" Mina asks.

"It's my favorite rule," Hollis says, talking over everyone else.

"Yeah, cause you're a sadist," I say.

"So, everyone closes their eyes, Cap goes into the middle of the circle, and then, in no particular order, he has to kiss the person he is most attracted to, the person he thinks is most attracted to *him*, and the person he knows the least," Hollis says.

"The person he thinks—"

"Who he wants, who he thinks wants him, who he doesn't really know at all."

"Got it. Evil."

"Ingenious. Jackie Jenessen was a senior when we were in seventh grade. They're my hero."

"They have like ten thousand followers on Instagram now," Ruby says, trying to show Mina her phone.

"OKAY!" I stand up. "Let's get this over with."

Quinn has his hands over his eyes, but he has his fingers spread. I kick him, and he closes his eyes for real. I stand alone in the middle of the circle. Suddenly, I feel better. I feel alone. I finish my beer.

"Caplan always takes his time," Hollis says to Mina. "It's his little rebellion." She has her eyes closed and her head to the side, chin up. She smirks, waiting.

I walk around the circle, a swing in my step now. I take Quinn's beer from him and finish that, too. Then I hand him the can.

"Cap, get down to it."

Usually when we play, I just kiss Hollis and then sit back down, since no one will know the difference, anyway. I turn to look at her. I didn't know someone could roll their eyes while they're closed, but she does. I drop to her level and put my forehead against hers so I don't surprise her. She tilts up to kiss me, one hand on my face, but both of mine are in fists in front of me on the ground. I sit back on my heels. Mina is next to her, eyes closed, looking peaceful. She's playing with the bottom of her dress in both hands. Someone has put something white and sparkly on her eyelids. It looks like tiny shards of glass. I lean closer to see it better. I realize it's not white but pale blue, like her eyes. She scratches her nose absently. I reach out without thinking and touch the spot she touched. She opens her eyes. Her mouth parts in surprise. Like a magnet, like what goes up must come down, like the easiest thing I've ever done, I lean in.

16

Mina

For the first time in my life, my mind empties. Caplan is kissing me. I am kissing Caplan.

17
Caplan

I pull back. She is looking at me with blank shock. Her mouth is still open. Then she lifts her chin up like she's about to say something, and I can't help it and kiss her again.

"What the fuck?"

We break apart.

Hollis is staring at us. Everyone is staring at us.

"What the fuck?" Hollis says again.

My mind is working in half time. I'm still holding on to one of Mina's wrists. She unlocks my fingers and peels them off. Her hands are shaking. I don't know where to look. Someone giggles nervously. Hollis stands up, looking down at me. I try to speak, and nothing comes out. She picks up her shirt and leaves, slamming the front door.

"Holy shit," says one of the guys.

"What happened? My eyes were closed."

"Caplan. Caplan, come on." Someone is pulling me

to my feet, hands under my armpits. It's Quinn. "You gotta go after her," he says, leading me toward the door. I try to look back at Mina, but she's staring at a spot on the carpet.

Ruby's front door bangs shut behind me.

"HOLLIS!"

She does not stop walking.

"Hollis, come on. Wait."

"Wait?" she calls without turning around. "Wait for what?"

"Please!" I'm running and she's walking, so I catch up to her pretty easily. I try to touch her arm, and she twists away. "Please wait," I say again.

"What am I waiting for?" She turns around so quickly I almost bang into her. She's crying. Not in the way she normally cries. Her face is all broken and messy, working hard to stop it.

"I'm sorry."

"You're sorry."

"Yeah—"

"What are you sorry for?"

"I'm sorry for kissing her?"

"Why are you sorry for that?" she spits. "It was a drinking game. It doesn't matter."

"But you're upset."

She turns around again.

"Hollis, come on. Please—"

"No, *you* come on."

Now she's really crying, her chest moving too fast. My head is spinning, and I feel like everything is flying up off the ground around me, like a comic book disaster, like the tornado that takes them all to Oz. I try to put my arms around her, and she kind of lets me for a second, and then she pushes me back.

"I'm sick of this," she says. "How are you not sick of this?"

"Of what?"

"I'm sick," she says very slowly and clearly, "of you."

I can't think of anything to say. We look at each other for a long time. I want to close the foot of space between us, but I don't know how.

"That was humiliating."

"I'm sorry," I try again.

"Sorry for what? Tell the truth. What are you sorry for?"

"I don't—I don't know what you mean."

"Do you love me?"

"I—god, you know I have, like, trouble with—shit, Hollis, I'm—I love my mom and that's probably it, but that doesn't mean that I don't—you know—you're like— you're the most—"

"Do you love Mina?"

All my internal organs trade places. She waits. *No,* I think, *no, of course not. I'm not in love with Mina. No one said anything about love.* But the words don't come.

"Okay," she says. "Right. Okay." She doesn't seem angry anymore, but the new look on her face scares me more. Then she hugs me. I hang on to her as tight as I can. Out of nowhere, like a nightmare, I realize I'm going to cry, too.

"We're breaking up, okay?" she says, still holding me.

I don't say anything, because I don't know how my voice will come out. She pulls away.

"I thought I'd have more time, you know?" she says,

laughing a little, pressing the palms of her hands into her eyes. "Not that much more, but—I mean I thought you'd figure it out at like, twenty-five, earliest."

"Figure what out?"

She looks at me like she's sorry for me, and then realizes I guess that I'm also crying. She folds for a second. I've never cried in front of Hollis. I've never really cried in front of anyone. She reaches out, like she's going to touch my face, and then drops her arm.

"You have to let me go now," she says, glaring at the dark ground between us. "Okay?"

"Okay," I say.

"And I'm gonna forgive you. Eventually. Because. Well, yeah, for what it's worth, I loved you. I totally did. I only didn't say it cause you couldn't take it."

She walks away.

I stand there waiting, sure beyond belief she'll pause at the corner, because she always does when we fight, and then I'll follow after her, cause that's how it goes. Or at the very least, I think, she'll turn around one more time to say good-bye.

But she doesn't. She goes left at the corner, and then she's gone. Hollis's house is a straight shot down Brighton. She didn't need to turn. That's when I know.

18

Mina

I wait until the door snaps shut behind Caplan to breathe out. I know that everyone is still looking at me. I peek and catch Ruby's face in a ridiculous cartoon *O*. She shuts her mouth quickly.

"Well, that was dramatic," Quinn says from somewhere behind me.

People laugh, and the air rushes back into the room. Someone half-heartedly suggests we keep playing. I'm not sure if anyone does. The music turns on again. I feel the world moving around me in odd smudges of color. I realize I'm the only person still sitting on the floor, in a circle that doesn't exist anymore, so I get up.

"Are you okay?" Quinn asks me.

"Sure," I say.

"That was something," he says.

I shrug.

He throws his head back and laughs. "Every time I think you'll do one thing, you go and do the opposite."

I smile.

"See?" he says.

"I don't like that game very much," I say.

"Fair enough. Wanna get out of here?"

I try to raise one eyebrow, like Hollis, but I'm sure both go up.

"Not like that," he says. "I just meant I'd walk you home. Or we could stay?"

"No," I say, "let's go. Unless you want to go to that other party?"

He scoffs and leads the way out. We pause at the door. He cracks it and peers both ways.

"Yeah, they're gone. We can take Huron instead of Brighton to be safe, though."

We walk along quietly for a little.

"Okay," he says, "tell me what you're thinking. Or I'll guess and get it wrong."

I take his hand. I see the pit of his dimple out of the corner of my eye, navy blue in the night.

"I'm sorry you saw that," I say.

"I didn't really," he says. "My eyes were closed. Was there something to see?"

"No," I say, "not exactly. He just caught me by surprise."

"Well, yeah," he says. "No shit."

"What?"

"The look on your face!"

I try to throw his hand back to him, but he grabs mine again right after.

"Was that really the first time you guys have ever? I mean—"

"Yes," I say, "definitely."

He's still sort of chuckling.

"I have no idea why he did it," I say.

"I mean, come on." He pulls my hand up over my head and makes me spin. "I know why."

"Shut up."

"You shut up."

"No, you shut up."

We walk along happily. Or he seems happy. I have a funny feeling, like when I've left the house and definitely forgotten something at home but I can't remember what.

"Don't you have to teach your class tonight?"

"Oh, I got someone to cover it."

"How come?"

He squeezes my hand. "Don't play dumb, nerd."

"I can't believe you said *wanna get out of here*," I say.

"Holy shit, please forget that right now."

"Nope," I say, swinging our hands like a metronome.

"You know what I meant."

"I don't."

"Like I'm not trying to take you home and wine and dine you and fuck you or—"

"You're not?"

Our hands drop dead between us. The smirk slides off his face.

"It's okay if you're not," I say in a small voice that I hate.

"No, I mean, well, I just. Would you want to?" He says it looking straight ahead.

I clench against the tide of questions and hypotheticals that rise inside me. It has to be someone, sooner or later. Better sooner, better Quinn. Better than some stranger next year at college. Better than Caplan.

I surprise myself into stillness with the thought. My

brain splits into ten different roads, going ten different directions, some back in time, some up into the clouds, loop-de-looping through an imagined world where that is an option. I realize Quinn is several steps ahead of me, looking at me, waiting. On the ground, in the real world. On the sidewalk, with me.

"Yes," I say. "I mean, I think so."

He blinks. "Have you ever, you know, before?"

I start walking again. "Um. Basically not. I mean, no, not really."

"Oh?"

"No," I say firmly, "I haven't. You have, I'm assuming?"

"Right, yeah. Yeah, I have. Not with, like, that many people or anything—just, like, a normal amount—"

"You don't have to explain," I say. "I don't mind that you already have. That's probably good. That way at least one of us will know what's going on."

"For sure," he says. He stops walking, and I realize with a start that we're in front of my house. I look around, but Caplan and Hollis are nowhere to be seen. "Did you mean, like, tonight? Like . . . like right now?"

"Oh," I say, "I mean, I don't know where we'd—my mom might be awake—so—"

"Okay, cool," he says, looking a little relieved. "But eventually, yeah, I'm down."

"You'd want to?"

"Mina," he says, shaking his head. He puts his face in his hands. "Obviously, I fucking want to," he says into his fingers.

"Okay, cool." I say.

"Cool?"

"Awesome. Fantastic. Like, soon?"

"Yeah," he says. "It should be, like, not a big deal or anything, but it should be a special thing. For you."

"Oh god, stop it."

"We could even, well, yeah, soon sounds great."

"Even what?"

"Forget it," he says.

"No, tell me."

"You're gonna laugh," he says.

"I promise I won't laugh."

"We could, like, on prom?"

We stare at each other for a moment.

"You're trying not to laugh," he says.

"No, I'm not. Okay, yeah, a bit. But you just make me laugh, so that's not fair."

"I told you it was stupid," he says.

"It's not," I say. "It's classic."

"It's dumb."

"The classics are the classics for a reason, though," I say.

We stand there in the dark. I look at him, the shadowy planes of his face, the nervous lift of his shoulders, and think, inexplicably, of explaining the word *trite* to Caplan. How he said it isn't my fault that we're in high school.

"Let's do it," I say.

He wiggles his eyebrows at me.

"What?"

"Do it."

"Oh my god."

"We're gonna *do it*."

"Yes, I suppose literally, we are."

"On prom night!" He punches his fists in the air.

"Maybe!" I shout back.

"Okay, maybe!"

He sticks his hand out, and we shake. We keep shaking, and he doesn't let go. Then we're just holding hands again. We become aware at the same time of someone turning the corner, a tall weaving figure coming down Corey Street.

"We should—"

"Go, yeah," he says. "Actually, you go, I'm gonna stay for a second."

I run to my door, more quickly than I'm proud of. I slam it behind me and hope my mother is deep in medicated sleep.

When I get to my room, it's chilly and a mess. I've left the window wide open, my clothes are all over the mattress, and my quilt is on the floor. It's the first time in my life that I haven't had hours to fill, endless time to clean and straighten and keep each thing in its place. My whole life, Caplan has teased me about being anal, but the messy room gives me an odd pleasure. It looks like someone busy, someone always coming and going, lives here. I lie down on top of all my clothes and try to imagine having sex with Quinn. It's more than I'd hoped for, going to college having had sex in a normal way at least once. And kissing him so far has been nice.

Caplan kissed me.

Why on earth did Caplan kiss me?

I roll over onto my stomach and press my face into the mattress. It's not like I can compare the two. Caplan surprised me, so I didn't have time to think. When I kiss

Quinn, I am definitely thinking the entire time, *Is this right? Is this nice?* But there are far worse things I could be thinking. I realize, with a surge of dread, that I need something to wear to prom. Had Caplan kissed me just to follow the rules of the game? Which rule applied to me, then? I'm not the person he knows the least. I'm not the person he's most attracted to. That leaves the person he thinks is most attracted to him. An old familiar misery steals over me. He knows, of course he knows, because everyone knows. But he kissed me twice, I try to reason with myself. Definitively, two separate times.

Am I the person he thinks is most attracted to him *and* the person he is most attracted to? Or am I the person he knows the least? Of course not. We know each other best of anyone.

But do we really, if I'm lying here wondering why he did it and what in the world he'd been trying to tell me? Hadn't there once been a time when I would have just known? And if not, when had there ever been a single thing I hadn't been able to ask him? I shiver as a breeze blows the curtains in. Maybe, I think, maybe the second kiss wasn't a part of the game at all. Maybe he just wanted to. I go to slide the window down and freeze when I hear their voices, floating up to me.

19
Caplan

I have no memory of deciding to walk home. I just let my feet do their thing. Hollis used to say I was like a character in a video game, with infinite lives, popping back up at the same spot after they die. Good as new, ready for the next round, invincible. No matter how drunk I get, I always find my way home.

I realize, as I turn the corner, that I probably only ever made it home all those times because of Hollis. I also realize I'm on my street.

"Cap?"

It's Quinn, standing under the streetlight in front of Mina's house. For some reason, I think he'll come to me, but he doesn't. He puts his hands in his pockets and waits.

"Hey," he says when I reach him.

"Hey."

"Is Hollis okay?"

"We broke up."

"Oh." He peers at me. "You okay?"

"Yeah."

"Well, you look like shit."

"That's funny. Cause I feel great."

"You guys will be back on in no time," he says.

"Yeah. I don't know."

"Prom, latest. I bet you twenty bucks."

"Big spender."

"I bet you . . . If you guys don't dance at prom, I'll go reverse commando under my grad robe."

"Pants? No briefs?"

"Briefs, no pants."

We shake on it.

"So, what was that about?" he asks.

"Breaking up?"

"Kissing Mina like that, in front of everyone."

"I don't even know."

"Really?"

His hands are still in his pockets and his voice is casual, but he's looking at me carefully. "Cause, you know, I cleared this whole thing with you in the first place cause I had a feeling you might—you know."

"Might what?"

Quinn sighs.

My heart is beating very quickly, and I don't even know why.

"Cause if it's like that, just tell me now. Tell me now and I'll back off."

It pops, like the flash of an old photo in my mind: Mina in the kitchen, crying out with one arm up, incandescent with joy, talking loose threads, deep breaths, and Quinn.

"You don't think, maybe—you don't like her, right?" he asks.

"Right."

"Right you do, or right you don't?"

"I don't," I say.

"Why'd you kiss her, then?"

I shrug. I wish he'd just take the answer and leave me alone. "I dunno. Why do we do anything?"

"The fuck does that mean, Cap?"

"See, right, I was being an asshole. Maybe I got jealous for a second. I'm not proud of it. But yeah, that's all. I don't see her that way. Not for real. I—yeah. Never could."

"You're sure?"

"Yeah. I'm sure."

He nods at me.

"I'm sorry I did it."

"Shit happens," he says. "I kissed Ruby at the Halloween dance in sixth grade."

"When I was dating her?"

"Well, you'd broken up that day."

"I never knew that."

"I missed her mouth," he says. "Too much gas on the landing. But the point is I tried."

He claps me on the back and then heads off down the street, doing a little bell jump at the corner, and I can't help it, I have to laugh.

That night, I have strange dreams. I'm on a road trip, on a bus like the one I used to ride to soccer camp. It shrinks and grows as people get on and off. I have the sense that we're touring the country, and people leave one by one, state by state. None of the passengers are people I know, but I still feel bad each time someone goes. I wonder if I'm going to ride the bus to the end of the line. Maybe there is no last stop, and I'll ride forever. Then I hear voices, low and calm. I can't hear what they are saying, but I know it's my mom and Mina. I stand up to look for them, but I cannot find them anywhere on the bus. I look for them under seats and through a maze of legs and luggage. I realize while I search that I can only walk forward, to the front, not back.

I wake up sweaty and uneasy, with a dry mouth. The events of the night come back to me, and I roll onto my side in case I'm going to throw up. It passes. I push Hollis from my mind and focus on kissing Mina, since that situation is the only one that can maybe be helped. I should text her. Actually, I should walk to her door and apologize. I sit up, and the room tilts alarmingly. I can see the edge of my phone in the corner under the heap of my sweatshirt. Getting to it seems impossible. Then I realize that Mina actually is nearby, downstairs, with my mom. They talk quietly. My mom laughs. I try to understand them. My mom says—*I found it in his pocket. It almost went through the wash. I love* Chrysanthemum, *too.* Mina says thank you.

When I wake up again, the light is different, and my phone is vibrating from the floor. I stare at it and contemplate going back to sleep.

My mom opens my door.

"Hey, trouble."

"Don't do it," I say. She flips the lights on. "MMMMMgrh."

"You'll have to get up to turn them off again." She comes and sits on the edge of my bed.

"So what did Mina tell you?"

"Nothing," she says. "She just told me not to wake you up, but to let you know that she's on her way to see her grandparents, and she won't be allowed to check her phone at brunch on pain of death."

She hands me a glass of water and two Advil. I take them.

"You should open a window in here. It smells like despair."

"Can you?"

"Get up, hon. You'll feel better. Greet the morning. Afternoon." She pauses in my doorway. "Mina also said to tell you everything is okay. And not to worry."

"Hm."

"Do you want to fill me in?"

"Will you turn the lights back off?"

She does.

"Hollis broke up with me. Among other things. Yeah."

She sighs. She comes back over and pushes my hair off my forehead. Then she cracks the window. "I'm headed to the hospital. I have a double shift. Can you figure out dinner with Ollie? I'll be home for breakfast."

"Yeah."

"Take a shower. Take a walk."

"No promises. Thanks, though." I take another sip of water.

"Do I want to know if you made curfew?"

"I'm sorry."

"That's okay. One down."

"How do you know I owe anyone else an apology?"

She holds both her hands up. Then she leaves, shutting my door gently.

When I finally get up, there is another single Advil on the counter next to the shower waiting for me.

20

Mina

The sun makes my eyes water on the drive home. My dad's parents live in an assisted-living community called the River House, which seems more like a spa than anything else, in the village of Grosse Pointe Shores. That's actually what it's called. They seem, to me, to be very able-bodied. And busy. Busybodied. I blink in the glare and ignore the routine dread that being on the highway gives me. It's funny how you can get comfortable with a bad feeling. How it becomes your friend. I think about asking my mother for her sunglasses since I'm the one driving, but I don't really want to see her face.

When we pull into our driveway, I see Caplan sitting on the roof under my window. He waves. I get out of the car without waiting or speaking to her, glad, after all, for the excuse.

He looks over his shoulder at me as I climb out of my window. He smiles, sheepish. I sit next to him, with some space, but let my legs hang down next to his.

"So, did you mean it?"

"Which bit?" I say.

"Are we okay?"

His hair is wet and dark. I can smell his shampoo. He's wearing a washed red long-sleeved shirt, pushed up to his elbows.

"Of course we are," I say.

"More than I deserve."

"Well, maybe."

"Look, Mina—"

"If you start apologizing, I'll push you off."

"Well, you deserve an explanation. And I know I'm no good at this, you know, these kinds of conversations—"

"No explanation necessary," I say. "I get it. Let's agree to not talk about it again, okay?"

"That's sort of, like, against the spirit of no never-minds, wouldn't you say?"

"Could you do me a favor, just this once, and let it go? I know you want to talk about it even less than I do."

"Right."

He looks across at his house, at the sun, half there, half gone at the roof's peak.

"I know you said it's okay, but it doesn't, like, feel okay."

"Well, it is," I say. "I feel fine about it. Maybe you just don't feel okay."

He looks at me then, hurt and open.

I swallow, make my face nothing. "You kissed me and it didn't mean anything to you, so you feel sorry for me. But I'm telling you now that it's fine—that's it. It's done. Let's not be precious about it." I made sure to cry about it last night so I wouldn't cry saying it to his face.

He's still looking at me like he's working something out, figuring how to spin it for me.

"I'm sorry," I say, "but I don't want to talk about it anymore. It was a long day."

"How was lunch in Satan's fanciest circle of hell?"

"Oh, the usual."

"You don't get two passes in a row," he says.

I lie down on my back and look at the trees, full and green above us.

"All they did was talk about Yale. And when I would say I wasn't sure or try to bring up Michigan, they would laugh, like I was joking. They were going on and on about some granddaughter of their friend who's going to be a freshman. They want me to room with her. Her name is, I shit you not, Arabella van den Gers."

"She sounds like a party. What did your mom say?"

"Fucking nothing."

He lies down next to me. "Should we just run away together?"

I don't say anything. If I stretched out my fingers, they'd touch some part of him. I don't know which, though.

"They can't make you go," he says.

"I know that. But sitting there, it felt like they can. Actually, it feels like they already have. Like it's all set. At one point, my grandma even got all weepy and said my dad would be so proud if he knew I was following in his footsteps."

"What'd you say?"

"Nothing. I'm my mother's daughter."

"Don't say that."

"None of this would be happening if he were here."

Irritated, I wipe my eyes. "Well, who even knows if that's true."

"What do you mean?"

"I don't know. Well, they say the things you remember most often are the least accurate. Like, each time you revisit a memory, your brain changes things a little. So all my memories of him are probably fiction at this point. I have no idea what it would be like if he were here. Maybe he'd push Yale harder than anyone."

"I can't really picture that," he says.

"How would you know?" It comes out too harsh, but I mean it. I want him to know, even though it's illogical.

"I met him, remember?"

"Once, when you were seven."

"Well, yeah. But I did have like, an impression of your dad. Or sense of him, I mean. I remember seeing you two skating at Pond Lake the first winter I moved here."

"Really?"

"Yeah, you were teaching him some spin you'd learned. You had your arms crossed in front of you, and I remember it looked really good to me. Very professional. And he kept trying to do it and falling down. And you were getting frustrated with him a little. And then you tried to put his hands in place and show him how to do it and you both fell and you were both sliding around trying to stand up and falling again. And I could tell you were both having, like, such a good time. Then I think you took one of his hands and started going around him in a big circle, and he stayed in the middle, but he was turning with you. You were so pleased he was finally doing it. And then you spun faster together, you in a circle, him in the same spot."

For a moment, I'm too stunned to speak. "I don't remember that at all."

"I only do cause I was jealous. I remember I thought he seemed like . . . you know. Like a really good dad. I also remember you were wearing a scarf with stripes. It was blue, red, and yellow. I thought it looked cool. I wanted one like it."

"I think I remember that scarf."

He takes my hand. He grabs it quickly, but our fingers come together very normally. It is strange and gentle. This is not a thing we do. We lie there, looking at the leaves arching above us, now cool and blue in the dusk, bending in the breeze. After some time, I let go and fold my hands in my lap.

"Have you made up with Hollis yet?"

"No," he says. He's looking up and not at me. "No, I think this is it. I think it should be it."

"So much for my time in the sorority."

"What do you mean?" he says.

"Well, you get me in the divorce, obviously."

This makes him smile. "I get you." He turns his head, and then our faces are only a few inches apart.

"What was your word of the day, yesterday?" I say quickly.

"Incandescent."

"Hm. That's a nice one, actually."

"It's ridiculous. I'll never use it. Imagine me using it."

I laugh. "I can't."

He sits up. He pulls out his phone and checks the time.

"Wanna come over for dinner? Ollie and I are making spaghetti."

"That's okay," I say.

He notices me looking at his lock screen. It's a photo of Hollis as a little kid, a ballerina with strawberry-blond hair and one arched eyebrow. I have this bizarre surge of feeling for her. I want to text her and say something, but I don't know what. Then again, I'm sure Hollis doesn't want to hear from me.

"I guess I should change that," he says.

"I guess you should. See you tomorrow."

"That," he says, reaching out for the top of the jungle gym we've never taken down, maybe because my dad built it, maybe because Caplan always climbs it, "is my favorite thing you say."

"Caplan?"

"Yeah?"

I know it's cowardly to bring it up once he's already on the ground. "Maybe don't say things like that to me, about running away together."

He gapes at me.

"Just so I don't get the wrong idea."

I climb in and shut the window. I move around my room, cleaning everything up, making noise so my mom can hear me and know that I'm ignoring her. This gets boring pretty quickly. Being petty usually does.

Caplan and I don't often talk about my dad, but every year on September 22, which is the day he died, Caplan becomes very interested in planning to hang out. He never explicitly brings it up unless I do, and the whole thing always amuses me, since we hang out every day, anyway, but all things considered, the fact that I laugh on that day is more than the childhood grief specialist my grandparents insisted on paying for ever did for me. Mostly, she asked me to color my feelings. I can't really draw, but to her credit, when I started a game of tic-tac-toe, she played and didn't necessarily let me win.

In ninth grade, on September 22, we went to the diner. Caplan ordered his chocolate milkshake and then looked at me expectantly. Since we were little, I've ordered vanilla, he's ordered chocolate, and somewhere along the way, he got the idea to each drink half of our milkshakes and then mix the rest together. He called it *chocolate vanilla swirl* and maintained it tasted better than either flavor on its own. When our moms took us to the diner after fifth-grade graduation, I had asked him if he ordered both milkshakes for himself whenever I wasn't there. His eyebrows pinched together, and he said he would never come to the diner without me. I only really remember this moment because it came back to me the first time I saw a picture of him and all his other friends there in eleventh grade after a party, having a drunk feast. Hollis was sitting on his lap. They were sharing a shake with two straws. But freshman year, in September, there were still few places we ever went without the other.

"And a vanilla for her," Caplan said when the waitress tried to take my order.

"I'm not hungry," I said as she walked away.

"Sure, but I am, and I still want half and half."

"So you're gonna drink half of each and then mix them?"

"If it comes to that."

I don't remember what we talked about then. But

somehow fathers came up, and then I said, "So. Who do you think has it worse?"

"What do you mean?"

He knew what I meant, so I waited.

"Seriously?" He poked around with his straw. "I'm not answering that."

"Fine. Never mind."

"All right. Well played. You, obviously," he said.

"You think?"

"Well, you had a great dad, and I had a bad dad. You had more to lose."

"You still have a dad, Caplan."

"Not really," he said. "He never wanted to be a dad, so."

"That's not true," I said stupidly, not even fifteen, thinking I knew anything at all.

"Yeah, it is. He told my mom."

"He said that in front of you?"

"Well, they were yelling. And my mom said he could at least pretend he'd wanted to be a father." He stirred his shake. "I didn't hear his answer, but I can guess."

At this point, we were almost a year into Caplan physically pulling me through the days. I wanted to be able to do the same for him, if only for a second, but I didn't know how.

"Besides," he said, "people's parents split up all the time. Less than they, you know—"

"Get road-killed?"

"Jesus Christ, Mina."

"Sorry. That was a joke."

"You have a real gift for comedy. You should do stand-up."

"Yeah, right, me onstage in front of people." I un-wrapped my straw for something to do.

"You didn't used to mind. Remember the all-county spelling bee?"

"Yeah, well, I didn't used to mind lots of stuff. That's called *growing up*. Speaking of, I wanted to talk to you about homecoming."

"Oh, me, too, actually," he said.

"No, me first," I said. "I'm done. I'm putting my foot down. I've spent my entire prepubescent existence al-lowing you to sucker me into going to those godforsaken cult-adjacent archaic functions, but we're in high school now and it's not cute anymore. It's just sad. It is time for us to accept that we can be into different things and still be best friends."

"I love when you admit we're best friends." He had a chocolate mustache. That's how I see his face, when I remember him saying that. Fourteen years old, the choc-olate, and the collar of a red-and-white-striped rugby shirt, one side popped by accident. "And are you saying I'm into archaic cult functions?"

"Well, I get it. Your disciples all gather there," I said.

"I don't know what that word means, and I bet it's mean, so—"

"More mean to them than you . . ."

"What I actually wanted to talk to you about—"

"Though I guess the king of fools is the biggest fool of all—"

"I thought I'd ask a date this year." At this point, he'd wiped the mustache off. He was looking down at his glass.

"Ask a date?"

"Yeah, like, a girl." He realized right away. "Sorry, I mean, obviously, you're a girl. I meant, like, I might ask someone out to the dance. Not as a friend. So I just wanted to check with you, since we always go together, if you'd be fine with that, but it sounds like it's a win-win if you're sure you don't want to go, anyway."

"Oh," I said. "Right. Totally. Win-win. So, who's the lucky girl?"

"That's the other thing—"

"Are you asking Hollis or asking someone else to make her jealous?"

I knew I'd surprised him, which was ultimately an insult to my intelligence. Everyone who was paying attention knew they liked each other. They always had. As far back as I can remember, whenever Caplan did something particularly impressive with a soccer ball at recess, he'd look up to see if she was watching.

"I was thinking," he said, "in the spirit of honesty and maturity, I should just ask Hollis."

"That would probably be best."

"I'm sorry. I know she can be, you know —"

"A horror show?"

"She can be harsh. In a, well, performing kinda way. Okay, yeah, a horror show. I don't even know why I like her."

"Well, I do."

Hollis was a person who inspired action.

I can't specifically recall the decision to not speak at school anymore. I'm sure there was a period of time when certain teachers pushed back against it, but when my clear and chronological memories pick back up, most of them had simply stopped calling on me. Maybe

I had enough goodwill after all my years of occupational teacher's-petting. Or maybe my written work could speak for itself. I never missed a single class or a single assignment. I just refused to speak out loud to anyone but Caplan, his mom, and my mom. Then we started high school, and none of the teachers knew me any differently.

Once I stopped talking, my tormentors had to adapt their tactics, since I was now giving them so little to work with. I have to admit, they evolved brilliantly. "Mina, if you're a loser, say nothing," is obviously not the most advanced dig, but as a concept, it was foolproof. And it endured. "If you live in the psych ward, say nothing." "If you're so flat-chested the bra falls off, say nothing." "If you sleep hanging upside down, say nothing." "If you want us to hold you down and pluck your unibrow, say nothing." "If you're going Stephen Hawking on us, say nothing." I think that one was Quinn, actually. During the first week of freshman year, as we walked out of the girls' locker room for gym, Hollis called out from behind me, "If you're a deaf-mute virgin, say nothing."

The whole question of whether or not I was a virgin was deeply confusing and upsetting to me at that time, for obvious reasons. Somehow, this irrelevant offhand comment shocked me into defense and, by accident, speech. I said back, without turning around, "If you're a predictable bullying bobblehead, gasp now."

And I shit you not, she did. I couldn't remember the last time I felt that cool. Or the last time I felt cool at all, for that matter.

After that, she never openly made fun of me again, but the pleasure of this peace faded quickly. Hollis can ignore you like a scream. Like a punch in the face. That's how real it feels, even though she's not doing or saying a thing, when she looks straight through you. It's remarkable. It was around that time that I had to face facts—it didn't matter if she was torturing me or not. I'd still notice her. Everyone noticed Hollis. She was one of those people. She was hard to look away from. Like someone else I knew.

"You know why I like her?" Caplan said, finally pulling my vanilla shake toward him. "Because if you do, please tell me."

"Because," I said, "she's a person of consequence."

"I don't know what that means."

"She's that girl."

It was also during that same period of freshman year that I started talking again in school. Bit by bit, day by day. But in my memory, talking back at Hollis was the moment I broke through to the other side, which wasn't a place necessarily devoid of nightmares or panic attacks that would double me over; but it was a place in which a human girl could speak, eat, sleep, and wake, in spite of it all.

"Cheers," Caplan had said, raising his half-chocolate, half-vanilla milkshake to me. I looked down at my own and realized it was also mixed. I had drunk it without noticing.

While we walked home, Caplan asked who I thought had it worse.

"I guess me," I said. "Your logic is sound. Your situation is more common, statistically."

"Yeah, but that's not what you thought at first."

"Yeah, well, whatever."

"No neverminds, Mina. You thought it was me."

"All right, yeah, I did."

"How come?"

I remember my stomach felt odd. I hadn't been full in a long time.

"Come on," he said. "I can take it."

"Fine. My dad would be here for me, if he could be. I think. Yours is choosing not to be."

He looked at me for a long time without talking.

"I'm sorry," I said.

He nodded and looked down the street away from me. We were standing at the corner of Corey Street. The entrance to our little dead end of the wide world.

"That's the point of no neverminds," he said. "And so is this. Why'd you stop talking last year?"

This time I said nothing.

"And eating. And, like, smiling."

I shrugged.

"What happened to you on that vacation, over winter break last year?"

I was so surprised then that I looked right at him. I guess I shouldn't have been. I guess it was obvious to anyone who was paying attention. Maybe I talked in my sleep. Maybe he read my journal. Maybe you always tell one person, in tiny ways, every day, without realizing. And that's how you come back to life. As long as they're the right person. As long as they're listening.

As I'm pretending to clean my room, I pick up the library borrowing card that Julia gave back to me. She said she found it in Caplan's pocket and that it almost went through the wash. I told him it was garbage. It is garbage. Still, the fact that he kept it and that Julia saved it rooted me to the spot on their kitchen stool with relief.

My room is clinically neat, which depresses me a bit, so I move downstairs. I have this idea that I'll deep clean, so I guess I'm in the mood to be miserable, but instead, I end up looking at the fridge, scanning the Christmas cards to see his face, test myself, but it isn't there. I look behind the fridge, on the floor, in the trash. I'm looking even though I suddenly know Caplan got rid of it. The space on the fridge, oddly clean, where it used to be, confuses me. It is a gift, and it is a jarring hole. I use the magnet and hang up the *Chrysanthemum* borrowing card.

21

Caplan

The sun sets twice, that night, in Two Docks. Once for everyone else, at 9:15, while we lie on the roof. Then again, just for me, at 3:00 a.m., when her bedroom window finally goes dark.

I realize that this has been true for most of my life, without me noticing. I don't ever go to bed without at least wondering whether or not she has, too. If I've done this for ten years without worrying what it means, it shouldn't be too hard to go back to that.

The last two weeks of school are a joke, but a good one, usually. This year, it's a confusing blur. Each day has a different spirit theme. Each night is someone else's grad party. Monday and Tuesday, we take finals. Wednesday is Decades Day. Thursday is Twin Day. Friday is High School Movies Day. The next Monday is Senior Skip Day. Tuesday is Two Docks Team Spirit Day. Wednesday night is prom. Traditionally, that day, the seniors wear pj's, and everyone else wears tacky fancy stuff. Thursday, no more school. Friday morning, we graduate. And that's it.

I walk to school with Mina both days of finals. We quiz each other, Mina making me monologue everything I know about different revolutions and wars, and me reading her questions from the physics study guide, speaking a language I do not understand. If we talk, we talk about nothing, and the more normal she acts, the more insane I feel. Despite deciding to leave Quinn's way clear, I catch myself constantly trying to figure out how to spend more time with her, how to see her alone, how to touch her for even a second at a time. It makes me feel so guilty it's like a stomachache, but I don't stop, either. I feel out of time, and all the extra air has been sucked out of our lives. It's like someone sped up the clocks, and no one's noticed but me. We hardly get a real moment together. When we do, she is friendly and bright, but in a hard, closed way. I can't figure out how she is doing it. She isn't strange or cold, but she has also turned off the tap somehow. There is no space for me to do or say anything unusual. The plans—half-baked, selfish, and impossible—bang around in my head. I have whole imaginary conversations with her in my bed at night, trying to script what she'd say, and what I'd say, and on and on and on.

Each theme day brings some fresh hell. Well, besides Decades. That one's fine. I cop out and wear my varsity jacket. Quinn wears a toga, which makes no sense. Hollis dresses to kill, in a fringe suede jacket and knee-high white boots and tiny sunglasses. She oscillates between viciously ignoring me and randomly saying hello just to watch me jump. Mina ignores the theme on principle just as she always has.

On Thursday, I match with Quinn. That night is Becca's grad party, on the roof of the only niceish hotel in town. Becca un-invites me that morning, and then Hollis gets furious at her and she re-invites me by lunch.

"For your information," Hollis says to me in the hallway without turning around, "I didn't tell her to un-invite you."

"Oh, thanks."

"Because I don't care where you go or what you do."

"Want out of your prom bet?" I ask Quinn, who's walking next to me.

"I'm a man of faith," he says, "and happy endings."

"You're both idiots," Hollis says from several feet ahead, "and black hoodies don't count as twinning."

Mina isn't invited to Becca's, and I try to see this as an opportunity to relax and enjoy myself with my friends. I spend the entire night wondering where she is and what she's doing. There's no real dinner, just an endless stream of tiny gross food on shiny plastic trays, so I get wasted by mistake. There is a 99 percent chance she's at home reading a book, and if I leave now, I can go over and we won't be interrupted and Quinn will be busy here and I'll—

"You know these things wrapped in bacon are kinda lit," he says, popping one in his mouth.

"Those are prunes," Hollis says, appearing at the high-top table we're standing at. He spits it out into his champagne flute. She gives him a withering look and stalks off.

"What?" he says. "Don't they make you shit?"

I shrug.

"Fuck this party," he says. "Why is there nowhere to sit?"

Two minutes later, Becca sticks her head under the stiff white tablecloth Quinn and I have set up camp beneath.

"What are you doing under a table?"

"Um. Getting some air?" I say.

Quinn nods seriously, his mouth pressed firmly together.

"Are you hiding from Hollis?"

"Yes," I say, "absolutely."

She rolls her eyes and disappears.

Quinn lets out all the smoke in his mouth, coughing. I retrieve his one-hitter from my suit jacket pocket. Some of the weed has spilled. I pinch it up and make a little pile on Quinn's cocktail napkin, next to the mini shrimp and charcuterie. He eats an olive and uses the toothpick to clean out the pipe.

"Will you snag me another bacon thing?"

"You sure? No big plans later?"

"Nah, Mina's at that honors dinner," he says.

I suffer immediate indigestion at the fact that he knows this and I don't.

He opens his phone. She sent him a picture. I try to look without looking, but then he just shows it to me. She's standing in front of a shoddy stage decorated with green-and-yellow fake flowers erected in the cafeteria, holding an official-looking certificate with the words *Jane B. Emmett English Award* printed in script and mounted on a square of slick black leather. She's wearing a soft purple dress I've never seen before. It's got pockets and no straps. A girl stands next to her, in thick red glasses, who I vaguely recognize. She has her arm around Mina. They are smiling. Under the picture, she's texted Quinn—

> My mom took this lol
> I didn't have anyone else to send it to

"Who's that?" I ask, pointing at the other girl, just for something to say.

"That's Lorraine," Quinn says, "Lorraine Daniels."

"Ah, right."

"Yeah, they're kinda friends, but then she was shitty to Mina last weekend about, like, being social. With us. Sorry."

"Why sorry?"

"Just, you know, you already know all that, I bet. I just meant, I think it's cool of her that she presented Mina's award after being a dick. It's kinda classy. Nerd code of honor."

I turn Quinn's one-hitter over and over in my hands. "What—um, what was the award? That Mina won?" I ask.

He looks at me and then at his shoes. "An English award, for her final paper, I think."

"Right."

"What book was it on? Do you know?"

"Don't do that," I say.

"What?"

"It was comparing *Anne of Green Gables* and *Jane Eyre*," I mumble.

Then I exit with as much dignity as I can, crawling on my hands and knees.

For High School Movies Day, the plan, way back, was to dress up as Ferris Bueller, Cameron, and Sloan: me, Quinn, and Hollis. Since Hollis wore the fringe jacket already for Decades Day, I accept the not-so-subtle hint that she's out. I wonder for a second, as I put on the outfit she thrifted for me months ago, if Quinn will bail, too, since I was so weird with him last night. I'm tempted to ditch my costume, since I don't think I can stomach showing up in it alone, but I don't. On my way out, my mom reminds me to pick up ice from Quickstop on the way home.

"For what?"

"For tonight." She stares at me. "For the party?"

"Right, yes, got it. Do we need anything else?"

"No, Quinn's family handled the food. Maybe come straight home after school to help set up? I can't reach the top of the garage, and I got a very ugly banner we need to hang."

"Can do," I say. "Oh, also, I invited Dad. I mean, I sent him an email about it. I know he probably won't come, but just in case he does, I wanted to let you know."

She leans against the doorway and looks like she's about to say some brilliant mom thing I'd rather not hear, so I divert.

"Well, thanks for all the planning. And for taking off work."

"You only graduate from high school once. I'm not missing it."

I walk back up to the door and hug her.

She hugs me back with the arm not holding her coffee. "What's this for?"

"You've never missed anything, and I never say thank you."

"Yes, you do. You do every day, you don't even realize it. Now go or you'll be late."

I'm stretched out on the bench outside the main office when I hear the principal yelling from another hallway, something about safety violations and it not being too late for a suspension. Then Quinn explodes around the corner, skateboard in hand, in the classic Detroit Red Wings jersey. He doesn't break stride as he sprints past, but he gives me a salute before vanishing into the girls' bathroom.

The principal storms around the corner. He sees me on the bench. "Did you see Quinn Amick come this way?"

"No, sir, I did not."

He looks down at my costume for a few seconds, his brow furrowed. When it dawns on him, I swear he almost smiles. Then he tells me to hurry up and start the announcements.

When I exit, the hallway is crowded with people moving from homeroom to first period, taking their time, showing off, and posing for pictures. A small crowd has gathered in the general vicinity of Hollis's locker, and I prepare myself for whatever look she's pulled this time. I see Ruby, Becca, and the other girls off to the side, dressed as Heathers. There are too many of them for the characters. I don't remember a purple Heather. Then the crowd shifts and parts, and I see Mina, in a Two Docks High cheerleader's uniform, and Hollis, in what is unmistakably Mina's clothes: a plaid skirt, a sweater vest, knee socks, and loafers. They're posing together for a photo, standing side by side and holding hands, looking like the evil fucking twins from *The Shining*.

"What's with you?" Mina asks me as the bell rings and people start to disperse.

"Me? What's with me? What movie are you even supposed to be?"

"We're not characters, we're archetypes."

"You never do themes."

She shrugs.

"It was Hollis's idea. I thought it was funny."

"Hollis isn't even a cheerleader."

"Yes, I know that. I borrowed this from Ruby."

"What happened to *I get you in the divorce*?"

"Lighten up," she says, heading down the hallway. I follow her. "It's just for fun. I never dressed up for the themes because no one asked me to."

"Because you always said it was stupid!"

"Well, I'm opening my mind and trying new things."

"Yeah, clearly."

"What is that supposed to mean?" She has her hands on her hips. She's got makeup on, and her hair is gelled into a tight ponytail, the way Ruby wears it for games. I press my hands into my eyes as if this is all some terrible dream, a sick joke, and when I open them, Mina will be standing there as herself again.

"You're letting Hollis manipulate you," I say. "Why?"

"How is she manipulating me?"

"She's doing this to fuck with me! She's using you."

Mina's face turns to stone, and I genuinely take a step back. "Is it so impossible to consider," she says, "that not everything is about you?"

"Jesus Christ—"

"Or that someone besides you wants to be my friend?"

She goes into first period and leaves me standing there.

Hollis posts the photo of her and Mina on Instagram. I look at it and look at it and look at it until I get my phone confiscated.

22

Mina

Quinn whoops as Hollis and I come out of the caf doors. I try to turn around and slip back inside, but Hollis grabs my elbow and drags me forward. It's been a long day and it's only lunch. I can't tell if I'm having fun or if I want to go home and get into bed forever. But I've decided that tapping out would prove Caplan right or confirm he has successfully embarrassed me. Which he has. I feel so angry at him, and I can't even home in on one specific reason.

"Sorry," Quinn says, ducking his head and grinning at me when I get to their table. "Can you blame me?"

Actually, I can. I can home. Kissing someone you *could never see that way* is evil behavior. Worse than that, it's stupid. Worst of all, the kiss has lodged in my brain like gum in my hair, and the more I try to get rid of it, the stickier and messier and stranger it becomes. If that's how it felt, to me, to kiss someone who was just testing and confirming they have no ounce of attraction to me, something must be medically, emotionally wrong with me. I must experience everything all wrong, through a broken lens that reverses everything. But what else is new.

"Come on." Ruby takes me and Hollis by the hand and has us sit up on the table. She arranges the boys on the bench in front. "Last one, I promise," she says as they bitch and moan.

"It's too late to go into the yearbook, anyway," Quinn says from where he's lying on the ground across the front of the group.

"But you'll be glad in twenty years that we took this," Ruby promises.

"Where's Caplan?" someone asks.

"Detention, I think?"

"Should we wait?"

"No, the whole yearbook is gonna be an homage to him, anyway."

I get a sick twist in my stomach. What am I doing here? What am I trying to prove? How am I going to look back on this someday and not feel humiliated that for thirty seconds at the very end of high school I pretended to have friends?

"You know, you've always been this person," Hollis says, looking forward for the photo, chin down, hardly smiling. "That's pretty amazing."

"What do you mean?"

"Remember when we called you a witch in fourth grade and then you dressed as one for Halloween? That's why I knew you'd say yes to this."

I can't decide if I see the connection, but the idea makes me feel better.

"It wasn't, like, overkill, was it?" Hollis says after the photo call is finished. "That I Instagrammed us?"

"Did you?"

"Oh, right." She takes out her phone and shows me the post. "You know, we really need to make you an Instagram before you leave for college. We'll keep it low-key, a prom picture, a baby throwback, just something so potential friends know you're normal."

I barely hear her because I'm staring at the photo. Hollis and I stand in front of her locker, holding hands, halfway between glaring and smirking. I didn't know I could make that face. I didn't realize my belly button was out, if I stand up straight. Someone's hands stick in at the edge of the frame, clapping for us.

"We're the same height. I never realized."

"Is it okay?" she asks me. "I can take it down right now—"

"No! Don't take it down." I put my head in my hands.

"Are you overwhelmed," she asks, "because you look so fucking cool?"

"Yeah, I think so," I say into my hands. It makes her crack up. "I just don't know how to act."

She shrugs. "Just play the part. Act like a badass."

"How am I supposed to do that?"

"I don't know. For one thing, chin up, tits out," she says.

"That's two?"

"And whenever I'm feeling like a pussy or a fraud, I make myself do something that scares me, so then I can feel like a proud, hot bitch."

"You should put that on inspirational classroom posters."

. . .

After lunch, we walk back inside together, and I try to focus on the first part of her advice, if not the second. I find, much to my surprise, that it kinda works.

"I can't believe you walk around like this all the time," I say.

"I recommend only six to seven hours a day of it. Otherwise, you'll get a god complex."

"So what are you pushing? Eight to ten?"

She flicks me in the arm. My phone vibrates.

"What?" she says when I stop walking.

"Nothing," I say, putting it back in my bag.

"Is Caplan throwing a fit? Confessing his love?"

"No. No, of course not."

"Well, it's coming. Mark my words."

Her face betrays nothing when she says this. I have no idea if she's messing with me, or testing me, or performing some act of girl code so far above my head I don't even know the words to name it.

"It's not," I say. "Trust me. I heard it firsthand." She looks ready to ask more questions or double down on the subject, so I change it. "That was just an email from some alumni woman who interviewed me for Yale."

"Why's she emailing you?"

"Who knows," I say.

"You don't want to go, right?"

I look at her. "Did Caplan tell you that?"

She snorts. "You glitch every time someone mentions it. You skipped College T-Shirt Day."

"I was sick. I had a doctor's note and everything."

"Mm-hm."

"Fine. Yeah. I don't wanna go. But it's too late."

Do I mean this? Am I really this passive? Or this

tragic? Maybe I'm the one testing her. If I am, she passes with electric flying colors.

"Are you shitting me, Mina? We haven't even graduated yet. People transfer halfway through, like, sophomore year all the time. Or they take gap years. Or they drop out and invent something or publish the next great American novel and become rich and famous. There are no rules, and it's never too late. You can do whatever you want."

The hallway traffic has thinned. We don't have our next class together, and I know I need to turn around and walk to French, but I don't.

"God, all right." She takes my hand and pulls me into the girls' bathroom. A few sophomores are leaning on the sinks, talking.

"Go?" she says. They scamper. "So who have you told that you don't want to go to Yale?"

"Um. Caplan? And my mom, but she becomes instantly hard of hearing whenever I bring it up."

"And who else?"

"Well, you. Just now."

"Okay. Why don't we call the school and tell them?"

"Call—call the school?"

"Yeah. Why not?"

"Because—because we can't just—it's probably really complicated to find the right number and—"

"Here it is." She's holding up her phone. She's on the Yale Admissions website, on a page that says *Contact Us* in cool blue letters. "Want me to dial?"

"Oh my god." I slide down the side of the bathroom stalls.

"Okay, no dialing." She sits next to me. "But what

would happen if you did call and rescinded your acceptance? Hypothetically."

"Well, they'd probably have to deal with the money,
and then my grandparents would find out."

"And then what?"

"And they'd be upset."

"And?"

"I don't know. That would be hard for my mom."

"Do you think she'd want you to go to the wrong
school because of that?"

I think about it. "No," I say, "I don't. I mean I hope
not."

She sighs. "I see the difficulty of your situation."

"Thank you."

"But let's admit here and now, just between us, that if
you don't want to go, you're not going. So eventually the
unpleasantness of dealing with it all will come to pass.
Do you agree?"

"Yes," I say slowly, "I agree." And it's funny because
the words mean nothing. I can easily walk them back,
and yet as soon as I say them, I feel better. Less tight inside. Another loose thread.

"Good," she says, "that's a start. And since you already agreed to do something that scares you today—"

"I never agreed to that—"

"Let's tell someone else, right now. Someone other
than your family or your frenemy."

That gets me to laugh. "I can't call the school without
warning my mom."

"All right. So let's respond to this alumni woman and
tell her. She doesn't work for the school, right?"

"What's the point of that?"

"It's a step in the right direction."

I open the email. The woman's name is Diana Morano. I barely remember our conversation when she interviewed me. I skim. She's congratulating me and asking me something I don't quite understand about my essay.

"Doesn't matter what she said," Hollis says. "Just respond and let her know you're not actually going to Yale, but thank her for all her help and support or some shit, and say, 'Have a great summer, all the best, Mina.'"

I do as she says. I stare at the phone. I know I've just said there is no point, but suddenly I feel that there is, and that I'll set something in motion I can't take back.

Hollis looks over my shoulder. "Looks good to me," she says. "Want me to send it?"

"What?"

"Sometimes you need a friend to hit Send."

"Okay." I hand her my phone.

"You sure?"

"Yes. I'm sure."

She sends the email. It makes that woosh—a wonderfully free and finished sound, I realize.

"Well, that's that," she says, handing my phone back and standing up. "Good shit."

I want to hug her or cry, but I don't want to make it weird.

"So," she says. "What's this firsthand source you have about Caplan's feelings for you?"

"Do you really want to talk about this?" I ask her.

She thinks. Her face relaxes out of its terrifying cheekboned armor. "I guess not really," she says. "But I like you. It was an accident. I didn't mean to. But it's too late,

I already do. And now I'll be so mad if I can't be your friend because of him."

"Well," I say, "you don't need to worry. My window was open, and I heard him telling Quinn he could never see me that way."

Hollis considers this, leaning back against the stall and looking up at the ceiling.

"You know, we played hot seat at a party this fall, and I asked Caplan what his biggest regret was. Without even having to think about it, he said it was getting everyone to bully you in elementary school."

I start to laugh. "That doesn't make any sense."

"I know. He was so serious and noble about it, I didn't have the heart to tell him I was bullying you way before he moved to Two Docks."

"Do all boys think the world revolves around them?"

"Honestly, I think everyone does. At least everyone our age. But my point is, Caplan has a bit of a hero complex."

We sit there for a moment. I mull over what this means and how it connects to what he told Quinn.

"Why'd you tell me that story?" I ask.

"Cause it was one of the moments I knew that he loved you. In, like, all the ways. And if he didn't realize it yet, he would someday."

She says it with such finality that I don't have anything to say back.

Then she stands up. "We should go to class, I guess." She looks in the mirror and puts on lip balm.

"We'll get late slips."

"So? Don't tell me it'll be your fifth?"

"Well, no." I shuffle my feet. "Actually—"

"Oh my god—"

"Stop. It's not like it even matters to me—"

"You're joking, Mina."

"It just seems a shame, like so close to graduating."

"Will it be your first this year?"

"It'll be my first in four."

She throws her head back laughing.

"Come on, loser." She hooks her arm through mine. "Say you were bleeding. Say you were bonding. Chin up, tits out, and no one will question you."

23
Caplan

I don't realize how afraid I am that Mina might not show up to my grad party until she does. And then she is there, early, as always, pushing open the back door with her hip and carrying a tray of brownies. She's wearing a white dress with little red flowers around the bottom, and she's washed the gel out of her hair. It's all loose around her face, with two tiny braids in front. She looks like one of the hot elves from *Lord of the Rings*. I go up to her and take the tray.

"I had it," she says, but she still follows me. I'm trying to set it down when my mom takes it from me and moves it somewhere else. Mina hands me a package I hadn't noticed under her arm, wrapped in tissue paper.

"Happy graduation," she says. It is a knit scarf with blue, red, and yellow stripes. It looks old but clean, and it's very soft.

"That's an odd gift for June," says Gwen, Mina's mom, coming up to us.

"Oh, these two," my mom says, "they only make sense to each other."

I still haven't said anything, so Mina takes the scarf and wraps it around me.

"I can't take this," I get out.

"It's impolite to refuse a present."

"Mina."

"I want you to have it, and if someday I want it back, I'll just ask for it, right?"

I hug her.

"I'm gonna go put it somewhere safe," I say.

I want her to follow me, so we get a second alone. I want to say sorry for, I don't even know what, for all of it, in no particular order, but Ollie needs her help plugging in the music. Then when I get back, Quinn and his family are arriving, and Mina is shaking everyone's hand and I wonder if he's introducing her as his girlfriend and I suddenly don't feel sorry at all. I hover on the back steps, like a stupid little kid in time-out, and then Quinn calls me over. The parents take some pictures of us, and I try to remind myself that none of this is really his fault. Then he reaches out a hand for Mina, who says, "Oh, no, no," shaking her head, but my mom ushers her forward. She comes to stand in between us, and we take a humiliating photo I hope I never have to see. I go inside to pull myself together. I try to take some deep breaths, and when that doesn't work, I slip a beer from the cooler waiting in the kitchen. By the time I'm back, more people are arriving, and I lose track of both Quinn and Mina in the crowd. When I wander inside for a break, my mom is there.

"Help me?" She nods at the cooler. We each pick up a side. "So why didn't you mention Quinn and Mina?"

I resist the urge to drop my end. I shrug.

She's navigating down the steps backward, looking over her shoulder. "Are they an item?"

"An item?" I scoff.

"Wow. Okay. Sore subject?"

"Nope."

"So they are dating?"

"Ask them," I say.

She doesn't say a thing, but her expression makes me feel like shit.

I know Hollis will show up, cause she never misses an opportunity to disrupt my peace, but when she arrives with both her parents, neither of whom I've seen since we broke up, they're all incredibly kind. Her mom gives me a real hug. Her dad is scary, but then he always was. Hollis herself rolls her eyes at me and then straightens my collar and says, "Well, congratulations." I'm trying to figure out what to say back, some way to thank her for coming, for still being here, but then she steps to the side for other guests. I do my best to say hello to everyone and to thank them all for coming, to carry my hosting weight for my mom's sake. The folding tables draped in mismatched cloth groan under the trays from Meijer's, but I never make it over to try any of the food. Out of the corner of my eye, I can see Mina on the hammock with her mom, sharing a plate of dessert. I hope it means they've made up and that they've come to some kind of understanding about college. I vow, all bullshit aside, to ask her about it as soon as I can.

Sometime after it gets dark out, when people have started to dance in the driveway, Quinn's older brother slips me a flask with a wink. It's engraved with the word

Dumb. I have a feeling *Dumber* is around here somewhere, but I haven't seen him in a while, and I'm tired
of talking Michigan football with other people's dads, so
I go looking.

I find him with the other boys at the end of the driveway, passing around his flask, which does indeed say
Dumber.

"So, is tonight the night?" Noah asks.

"Nah, we're thinking prom."

"Why wait?"

"What's prom?" I ask.

Quinn looks at me, but everyone else is too busy falling over themselves, laughing. "Nothing—"

"A fucking fairy tale, a virgin on prom night."

"What?"

"Maybe not like, at prom," he says, shaking his head,
but he's loving it, "maybe after."

"Start the engine at prom, though," says some older
guy, one of Quinn's brother's friends. He makes a gross
gesture with two fingers, and even before I understand
what he means, my knuckles turn white on my flask.

"God, wonder how she'll be."

"Stiff as a board."

"No way. She's a freak. I can always tell."

"Hey, I'd take stiff. Then you know she'll be tight."

It isn't Quinn who says it, but something splits open
inside of me. He's laughing along, not looking at me,
when I shove him. He falls into the trash cans. One of
them rolls, spilling garbage in a perfect arc.

"What the fuck?" he says, looking at his scraped hands,
getting to his feet.

No one is laughing now.

"Cap, we're just messing around," someone says.

My hands are shaking. I push through them and walk farther up the driveway.

"Hey!" Quinn yells after me. "Look, if you're jealous, that's fine. Just talk to me about it. Don't fucking—"

"If that's how you're talking about her," I say, working to keep my voice even, "I don't want to talk to you."

"Oh, are you fucking kidding me?" Quinn laughs terribly. "You're too good now to talk about girls? Since when, Cap?"

"BUT IT'S MINA." I turn around. "It's Mina, and you can't talk about her like that."

"Mina isn't some weird different species, Caplan."

"And you can't just—just have sex with her." I'm forcing myself to whisper. I wish the other guys would fucking leave.

Quinn stares at me. Then he says, in a normal voice, "I mean. I can. If she wants to."

"She doesn't fucking want to."

"Yes, she does. We talked about it."

"But if you pressure her—"

"I'm not fucking pressuring her, oh my god—"

"No, you don't get it." I know I'm being too loud, and the boys are all listening, but I feel myself spinning out. "You don't understand."

"I can just tell, okay? I can tell by the way she acts when we hook up, by her body and her breathing and stuff—"

I hit him as hard as I can in the face. He staggers backward, with one hand over his eye. We look at each other with matching shock. I think he's about to break down, and then he swings his other arm and hits me in the nose.

"Okay, fuck this," Noah says, "I'm getting someone."

A sick white pain forces my eyes closed. I try to think what it feels like, to lodge myself in some familiar comparison, but there are some things, I guess, that don't feel like anything else.

"What don't I understand?" Quinn is yelling at me. "You think you have some fucked-up claim over her? Some magical connection, just cause you both don't have dads? Because that's bullshit, Caplan. Your dad isn't dead. He just left."

When I open my eyes again, there is blood all down my shirt. It's the button-down my mom bought me for graduation, I think, and then Hollis is there.

"Oh my god," she says. "Oh my god. Come on. Now. Stand up, Quinn. Yeah, I'm sure it fucking hurts. Get up now."

She drags us both to my front door.

"I'm fine," I say, "stop it."

"I'm fine, too," Quinn says.

"Grow up, both of you. You're not fine."

"Fuck off," he says, shoving her away. He stomps off to the driveway.

"He's mad at me, not you," I say to her.

"Yeah, no shit."

I try to inch away from the door. "It doesn't even hurt," I say.

"Caplan, you're covered in blood. If you go back now, you'll cause a scene."

I'm still resisting, but she's got my wrist in her hand.

"You'll upset your mom."

I let her bring me inside and straight upstairs to the bathroom. She has me take my shirt off, and then she starts to clean me up. I slip the flask from my pocket and take a sip. When she protests, I say, "My face fucking hurts, okay?"

"Well, you said you were fine."

"Well, I'm *not*."

Something in the way I say it gets her to drop it. She's just starting on the blood in my hair when someone calls my name. I stand up.

"It's fine—"

"That's Mina," I say. I push past her.

Mina is storming through the house. She stops when she sees me on the stairs, shirtless, still pretty bloody.

"What did you do?" she says.

I open my mouth, then close it again.

"What did you say to Quinn?"

"I just—I don't—"

"Caplan." Her voice is as hard as ice. "Tell me now. What you said to him."

"I—well, they were talking, the guys, about prom night, and about him and you, and I just—"

"What did you tell him?"

"Nothing!"

"Well, you told him something, because he dumped me."

All the air leaves my body. "He . . . he dumped you?"

"He said—he said you'd made something clear to him, and we had to stop, and we shouldn't go to prom together anymore." Her voice is rising, and I can't help but go to her. "You told him," she says, pushing me away with both hands. "You told him about me, about everything, and now he's freaked out."

"I didn't!" I stumble backward as it clicks—what she's accusing me of.

"Well, what else, then? What else did you *make clear to him*—"

"I just lost it, okay? And I didn't like how he was talking about you, and I just—but I would never tell anyone that, Mina, you know that."

"Then *why*," she says, pushing again, "why did he dump me?"

"OH MY GOD!" Hollis yells from behind me. "That's enough. You, come here, yes, yes, I am sure Caplan did something stupid, but there is no point in guessing. Sit." She sits Mina down on the bottom step. "And you," she says, "you, too. Now don't talk. Don't yell. Don't touch each other. Don't *hit* each other." She glares at me. "Just sit still."

"You can't put us in time-out," I say.

"Watch me."

"Where are you going?" Mina asks.

"I'm going," Hollis says, "to get Quinn. So we can ask him what happened."

I stand up. "I don't want to see him!"

"SIT."

24

Mina

Caplan and I wait on the stairs in silence. After a minute, he holds out his flask to me.

"Are you trying to be funny?" I shift away from him and pinch the inside of my upper arm to keep myself from unraveling.

When Hollis returns with Quinn, he looks exhausted. His eye is already swelling. He looks at us, sitting on the stairs like children. "Your mom's looking for you," he says to Caplan's knees.

"He can go in a minute," Hollis says. "Why did you end things with Mina? Did you do it because of Caplan?"

"Yeah," he says.

"What did he say to you?" Hollis asks.

"He didn't have to say anything. It's just obvious."

A sob crawls up my throat. As a person with a long list of fears, this is my greatest—that other people can tell. They can sense the broken part. They can smell it on me.

"What?" says Hollis, looking right at me. "What's obvious?"

Quinn takes a deep breath. "That even if they don't know it, they're eternally in love with each other and shit, and I'm bowing out, okay? I can't handle it. It's too much for me. This vibe is, like, not normal at all, I want you guys to know. This soap opera shit. It's completely wack. And I'm sorry, I really am sorry, Mina, cause I think you're so cool, but you guys just need to shut up and be together because you're making everyone around you miserable, including yourselves, and I can't be part of it anymore, okay? Maybe you were right. Maybe I just want to go to prom alone in a clown suit. Fucking sue me."

A long silence greets his words.

"I'm sorry about your face," Quinn says to Caplan. "And I'm sorry for laughing when the guys said gross things about you," he says to me.

"What did they say?" I ask.

"You don't want to know," Hollis says. "Trust me. From experience."

"They were saying, well, pretty graphically, that you'd be a good fuck."

"And you were doing what, exactly?" I stand up to better look down at Caplan. "Defending my honor? Well, maybe I *would* be a good fuck."

I have no idea what makes me say this, but now I'm really going to cry. I feel it rising in me, and I have no sense of what else will come pouring out.

They call after me as I run away, but I throw myself out the front door and across the street, into my own house, up the stairs, and under the covers, where I sob and sob and sob until there is nothing left in me. I cry like I did when I was small, when you can't speak yet, so you just make noise—animal sounds, as loud as I can, because no one can hear me. Everyone is across the street, a world away, at a beautiful party for my oldest friend. My only friend, who knows too much about me; who knows everything and cannot help but want to shield me from the rest of the world, from regular people—or more likely, shield them from me.

I roll over hours later, feeling soggy and pathetic and all wrung out, to my phone buzzing somewhere in the blankets. I ignore it, and then it starts ringing again. When I dig it out, I see Hollis's name lighting up the screen.

"Hi?"

"Hey, I'm sorry, but I need your help."

"What's wrong?"

"I couldn't think who else to call," she says.

"Are you okay?"

"Yes, I'm fine. It's Caplan. Can you come outside? We're down the street."

"I'll be right there."

I put a sweatshirt on over my dress and don't even bother with shoes.

They're not hard to find, because Caplan is making horrible gagging sounds. When I get to them, I realize nothing is even coming up. Hollis is behind him, trying to keep him sitting up with both her hands under his armpits. She looks awful. Her dress is covered in vomit.

Caplan's head rolls around on his neck. I kneel in front of him and try to help her keep him upright. His eyelids flutter, and when he sees me, he starts crying. His head falls forward onto my shoulder, and he's heaving all over me, incoherent.

I look at Hollis and she looks at me. "What happened?"

"I don't know," she says. "After you left, I told him to put on a clean shirt, and come back to the party, and keep it together."

Caplan cries harder on me, pushing into me so that I almost fall back into the street.

"And?"

"And he did the first two things, and then I guess he drank that whole stupid flask Quinn's brother gave him. I found him in the bushes, throwing up on himself, but he was still sort of with it at that point, and I got him to walk down the street with me so his mom wouldn't see him. But now it's past his curfew and she keeps calling his phone, but I can't get him to stand up."

Caplan is dry-heaving again, on his hands and knees.

"Okay," I say. "Okay." I get on one side of him, and Hollis gets on the other, and we pull him to his feet. We sway for a minute.

"I'm sorry," Hollis says.

"Don't be," I say.

"All right," she says. "Come on, Cap. Let's walk."

His knees buckle, and we prop him back up.

"He didn't even answer," he moans.

"It's okay," Hollis says. "You're okay."

We inch down the street, basically carrying him.

"When in god's name"—I'm completely out of

breath, though we've only walked twenty feet—"did he get so huge?"

"This is why boys don't get to be damsels in distress," Hollis says, panting. "It's an issue of physics."

"He didn't come," Caplan says again.

We get him up the steps, and his feet seem to be working slightly better.

"It'll be open," I say, "if Julia knows Caplan isn't in his bed."

But Hollis is already reaching for the knob. I realize she'd know that. Of course she would. She knows this house, its rhythms, and this boy more intimately than I do.

We get him over the threshold, shushing him and regaining our bearings, when a light at the top of the stairs flips on. Julia stands there in her pajamas, looking down at the three of us. She takes in the scene, Caplan barely conscious, Hollis and me struggling to hold him up. Hollis opens her mouth to say something, and Julia holds up a hand. She comes down the stairs and takes him from us. He falls into her arms, giving her all his weight.

"Dad," he cries. "Dad never answered. He never even answered."

Somehow, superhumanly, she leads him up the stairs.

At the top, Julia turns back to us.

"We're so—" Hollis says. "Can we—"

"Thank you," she says. "Go home, now. Your own mothers are probably worried."

When we get to the curb, Hollis collapses and puts her head between her knees. At first, I think she's crying, but then I realize she's laughing. I sit down next to her.

"As if my own mother is worried," she says. "They lock the door at midnight whether I'm home or not."

"Where will you sleep?"

She shrugs. "I'll call one of the girls till they wake up. Or I'll bang on my door till someone gets me. What are they gonna do, ground me? We graduate next week, and then I'm gone."

"You could sleep at mine?"

She looks at me. "Really?"

"Yeah," I say. "I mean, you're already here. And you could take a shower. You stink."

"Well. You look like you cried yourself to sleep."

"No shit."

"Could I really shower at two in the morning?"

"Sure," I say. "My mother isn't up worrying, either."

"June of senior year is like Neverland," Hollis says, once we're lying in my bed.

"How so?" I feel awake, even though it's 3:00 a.m. I guess because I took a nap at 10:00.

"Well, it's magical, obviously. All warm and sparkling."

"Sparkling?"

"Suddenly we're allowed to drink champagne. But it makes everyone act like they're never gonna grow up. When obviously that's exactly what we're all about to have to do."

I don't say anything for a moment. I feel ashamed. To think I've spent my entire conscious life observing Hollis, and I actually thought I knew her.

"You don't agree?"

"No, you're right," I say. "All the lost boys, dumping everyone and drinking too much and crying when it's not their turn to cry."

"Exactly."

"That would make you Wendy," I say.

"No, Mina," she sighs. "Try as I might, wish on whatever star, you're Wendy, and I'm fucking Tinker Bell."

I laugh.

She rolls over to face me, but her eyes are closing. "*Peter Pan* was my favorite growing up," she says. "What was yours?"

"Um. *Harry Potter?*"

"No, you and Cap shared that. What's one that was just yours?"

"Maybe *Cinderella*."

"Fucking classic."

We're quiet for a little.

"Her dad died, too," I say. "I think that's why I liked it. Which is corny."

"It's not," Hollis says. Then: "I wanted to say sorry, for saying that thing about your shoes in fourth grade."

"What?"

"When you used to wear the black Chucks every day and I said that thing about it being because your dad died—well, yeah, I'm sorry."

"That was you?"

"I mean, I really wasn't trying to be a bitch, for once. I had just read in a book, I think, that people wore black when they were in mourning, and so I was trying to tell the other girls to stop calling them boy shoes, but you heard me, and then you cried, and I felt terrible."

"That's okay," I say. "That's really sweet, actually."

"Yeah, that's me," she mumbles, "sweetest girl we know."

We lie there for a while.

I think she has fallen asleep, but then she says, "Okay. Now that we're friends—"

"Are we friends?"

"Yes, and now that we are—"

"Are you going to start singing 'Popular'?"

"Shut up and tell me a secret."

"A secret?"

"Yeah," she says, "something no one else knows."

"Okay. Well. The Yale woman emailed me back."

"What did she say?"

"She asked me what my plans were for next year. I guess in the first email, she was asking if I'd be interested in editing my college essay and selling it. Like, to publish it."

Hollis sits straight up in bed. "What do you mean? How'd she read it?"

"Well, a while ago, some college board person reached out and asked me if they could include my essay in a sort of guide about how to write them. Like examples or—"

"And yours was, what? The primo example? What did you write about? Life and death?"

"It was about nothing. I kept waiting for someone to tell me it wasn't good common app material. It was just about helping Caplan learn to read in elementary school. So, whatever, I guess that's how she read it, and her wife works for a literary magazine and they want to publish it, but then after I said I wasn't going to Yale, she asked if I had any interest in interning—"

"Oh my god, what'd you say?"

"I haven't replied yet."

"What's the magazine called?"

I get out my phone. "*The Nerve*?"

She gets out hers. "Oh my god. Mina. Their office is in New York. This is perfect. It'll be just like *Girls*. Look at the street view—"

"I can't just skip college and go to New York," I say. "I've never been. And I've never watched *Girls*. And I don't know anyone there."

"You'd know me," she says, offended. "And you're not skipping. You're taking a gap year."

"You'd pretend not to know me," I say.

"I would not. You completely seem like someone who's gonna blossom after high school. Not that you're not like—in bloom, now. Or whatever." She yawns and scoots down a bit under the blankets. "Get your toes away from me. They're freezing cold." Then, after a minute or two, she says, "I'm leaving right after graduation. I'm getting the fuck out of Two Docks and starting my real life. Come."

"Come?"

"That's what I said."

"You'd want me to be part of your real life?"

"Yeah. You could borrow my clothes."

I laugh. "Cause my clothes are so bad."

"No, they're not. I just love when people borrow mine," she says, snuggling down more. "Because I'm very arrogant and have amazing taste. I think it's like my love language or something. What's yours?"

"I don't know. Recommending books, maybe?"

"Thank you, by the way, for my birthday present from Caplan. I loved it. I've already restarted it."

I just smile, but her eyes are closed again.

"You should come to New York, Mina."

I don't reply.

"Are you pretending to be asleep?" she says.

"No," I say, "I'm thinking. You tell me a secret."

"I've been assaulted, too," she says.

"Oh—"

"Not to, like—"

"How did you—"

"I just thought, the way you cried at my birthday, it just had a certain look to it. That I recognized. That kind of crying, the way you were holding your knees. And then tonight, you said that thing about . . . about something you thought Caplan told Quinn. Maybe that's fucked up of me. I shouldn't have—I shouldn't have assumed."

"No, that's okay," I say. "I was, I guess. Assaulted. Too. Do—do I know who—"

"No," she says, yawning, leaning her forehead against my shoulder, "it was two summers ago, at camp. He was a CIT. I had the biggest crush on him when I was younger. What a waste of a superhot person."

I snort. "God, I'm sorry—"

"No, please laugh," she says. "It makes me feel fucking invincible to laugh at it."

"I think you are invincible, honestly," I say. "I always have."

"I'm really sorry about what happened to you," she says.

I roll over toward her and close my eyes. "I'm really sorry to you, too."

"Did you take Plan B? That was the worst part for me. Like, facing the camp nurse. She didn't even have it on hand, which I think is totally delusional at a co-ed camp."

"Oh, no, I didn't need to."

"So, even monsters use condoms?"

"No," I say. "No, I mean, well, I hadn't gotten my period yet. So."

Hollis says nothing. She searches with her hand under the covers until she finds mine. She squeezes it, then lets it go. Then she says, "Have you thought about it yet? About New York?"

"No. I mean, that was sort of . . . sort of a big thing you just brought up."

"Well. I'm moving in for the summer with other NYU girls. They said they have two rooms. The other one might still be open."

"Oh."

"Don't freak out. Just consider it."

"Okay."

"Okay. Good night, Mina."

"Good night, Hollis."

"Mina?"

"Mm?"

"I think you're invincible, too. I wouldn't want you to come if I didn't."

25
Caplan

I'm on the floor of the bathroom, locked in the fetal position, when Ollie opens the door.

"Mom says you live here now."

"Get out."

"She also says you have until 9:00 a.m. to get up and clean up all the vomit on the curb in front of the Morgans' house."

"What time is it now?"

"Almost eight."

I groan.

"I could do it for you . . ." he says.

I pull myself into a sitting position, using the rim of the toilet. "How much?"

"Fifty."

"Twenty."

"Thirty. And . . ." He tilts his head. "You have to make my bed every morning till you leave."

"For one week."

"Two weeks."

"How early in the morning?"

He thinks again. "Just has to be before I get back into bed at night."

"Deal." We shake. The motion makes me nauseous again. I rest my forehead back on the seat. "Mom doesn't care if we make our beds, you know. I never do."

"Yeah, well, you're sleeping on a toilet. I'm aiming higher than you."

"You can go now," I say. "You have vomit to clean."

"I like when my bed's made," he says. "It makes me feel good. You should try it."

He leaves, closing the door gently.

I lie back down on the tile and resume my staring at the dusty underside of the toilet bowl. It's not so bad here, I think. I can't mess anything up, from this exact spot. I can't let anyone down.

Eventually, the light grows brighter through the window, and I'm just considering standing up to pull the curtain closed when I hear the front door open.

"He looks like he crawled out of the ground," I hear Ollie say happily. "Go see."

I'm not sure who I'm expecting. I guess Quinn, but I don't look when the door opens.

"I heard you live here now," she says.

"I'm trying it out," I say.

"It's not so good. For a boy who loves roofs. And the tops of trees."

I roll over and look at her. She's standing in the doorway, holding a Gatorade and a box of saltines.

"Can I come in?"

"I'm not sure you want to," I say.

"Remember when we tried to sleep in a tent in your backyard and I got appendicitis and you let me throw up all over you in the car on the way to the hospital?"

I smile. The muscles in my face feel odd and stiff. Pain shoots out from my nose. Mina shuts the door behind her and sits down across from me, against the tub. She pushes the Gatorade toward me and wraps her arms around her knees.

"I don't deserve treats."

"Oh, stop feeling sorry for yourself."

I open the bottle and take a sip. To my surprise, it tastes amazing. I take another big gulp. Then I close the bottle and press it against my forehead because it's still cold.

"You're acting like you invented getting too drunk."

"Is our fight over?" I ask.

"I don't know," she says.

"But you're here."

"Yes. Because you're weak and vulnerable. So our fight is paused."

"My mom says you and Hollis carried me home."

"We had a sleepover after, actually."

"No way. Hollis hates sleepovers."

"It was weirdly fun. It made me feel better, about—I don't know. Kind of everything." She smiles at me. A real Mina smile, soft and sharp at the same time.

"No," I say suddenly. "No pausing the fight. No pity. Lay it on me."

Her eyes move slowly over my face and then my body. All at once, I feel very aware that I'm only in my socks and boxers.

"I can't," she says. "You're too pathetic looking. It

wouldn't be right." She reaches out and scratches at some old, dried blood on my collarbone.

"Mina—"

"I know. It's okay."

"It's not. I'm—I'm sorry. About Quinn."

"Honestly . . ." She leans back on the edge of the tub. "It's for the best. I think I was ultimately going to use him for sex."

I burst out laughing. "No way."

"Yeah, that was definitely part of it."

We're both cracking up now. I realize I'm starving, and I reach for the saltines.

"Just because I can't stay angry at you doesn't mean you shouldn't feel awful," she says.

"I do. I feel totally awful."

"I mean, it would have been nice to graduate having done it at least once."

"I don't believe it," I say. "You were just . . . just . . ."

"Horny?"

"Holy shit."

"Oh, grow up," she says.

"You were horny."

"Is that so surprising?" She rests her cheek on her arms, folded on her knees. There's a funny light in her eyes.

"No," I say, swallowing hard. "No, of course not, I mean, it's natural that you'd—that you'd wonder how it would—you know—feel."

"Are you okay?"

"Course I'm okay—"

"You're bright red."

"Am not."

"And I do know how it feels, mostly," she says. "No,

no not because of that. Obviously. I mean, I've figured out what I can, since. On my own. What?"

I open my mouth, and then close it, and then open it again, trying to remember the English language.

"Come on," she says. "Are you really so sexist about masturbation?"

"N-no, I'm—I mean, of course not. I just—"

"You do it, I bet."

"Well, yeah, I mean, but I just—"

"What, you think it's only for boys?"

"No, no. I know girls, women, I mean, can . . . can also—stop laughing at me!"

"You're being funny!"

"This is a crazy conversation!" But I can't make myself look away from her. It's the most she's looked at me in weeks. "You used to have panic attacks if people accidently touched you in the hallway!"

"Yes, well, that's different. I'm not other people. I can touch myself. Okay, close your mouth. You look ridiculous."

I do.

"I know I sort of fell apart right after it happened. And you saw the worst of it. But it's not like I didn't eventually try dealing with it on every level."

"What do you mean, on every level?"

She looks past me. "Like I know you were worried that I wasn't talking or eating or sleeping, but I was worried that I'd never be able to enjoy sex or that I'd never grow up correctly and want it, and I determined not to fall behind, you know, or not develop correctly, so I got a head start and did research and read books, and it took some time and practice, obviously."

"Pr-practice?"

"There are actually really amazing resources for girls now that didn't even exist a few years ago, things that aren't just, like, porny and gross—stuff that's very educational and unintimidating."

"Are you—are you saying you overachievered your way through—through jacking off?" She's laughing again, and I get defensive. "I'm just, give me a break, okay? This is new territory! We've never talked about this before!"

"Why in the world would we have ever talked about it? What, would you wanna tell me how many times a week you do it?"

"Well, sure, I would have, if you asked!"

"Okay. How many times?"

"Oh my god." I put my face in my hands.

"See?" she says, thrilled.

"Fine!" I yell into my hands. "Fine, can we please talk about something else? Can we go back to our fight?"

"Okay, okay," she says, "I'm done."

"With that conversation? Or our fight?"

"Both."

"Excellent."

We sit there on the bathroom floor for a moment. Now, for some reason, I can look anywhere but her face. I wish I were wearing pants.

"Want to take a walk?" she asks. "Those saltines are staying down. Maybe you could handle something more substantial."

"Sure," I say.

She stands up and offers me her hand.

I don't take it. My arms are crossed over my lap.

"What?"

"Nothing," I say.

"Come on."

"Be right there."

"Why, what's wrong?"

"I just need to, you know—I'll get dressed and be right there."

"Why are you being so weird?" she asks.

"I'm not?"

"Then get up." She reaches out to me again.

"No! I can't."

"Why not?"

"I just can't, okay?"

"You just can't?"

We stare at each other.

"Oh my god," she says.

"Stop it."

"Are you—"

I stare at her, and she stares at me. She puts her hand over her mouth.

I stand up with as much pride as I can muster, my hands folded in front of me.

"Oh my god. Oh my GOD!"

"WHAT? What do you want from me?! You came in here all looking all—and being nice to me, and . . . and talking about, about being horny, and about—you know—"

"Masturbating?"

"STOP! STOP SAYING THAT." I turn around, but there is nowhere to go in the tiny bathroom, so I just sort of spin in a circle and she's still right there. "I'm so sorry," I say.

"No," she says, "don't be. It's a compliment."

"Yeah. Yeah, it is."

She's pressing her lips together to keep from laughing. Then the thought comes, surging up, insisting on itself, even though it couldn't be less the time. I'm sweaty and sick in my underwear and have basically just peeled myself off the bathroom floor and desperately need to take a shower.

"Right," I say. "Let's just—you go, and I'll meet you downstairs."

But she doesn't go. She tilts her head to one side. Nothing on earth could make me look away now. I feel each beat of my heart like a gong in my throat. She looks down at my hands, still folded strategically. For a second that may be very long or very short, I don't know, I can't move or speak at all. She takes my wrists in her hands and pulls them apart. She looks there, then looks up at me. Then we're kissing. She puts my arms around her. Time speeds up, and we're pressing against each other so hard that I lose my balance and I think I pull the shower curtain off its rod. It falls on top of us, and she's laughing into my mouth and pushing the curtain away and kissing me more and then we're on the floor and she's throwing her shirt somewhere and we're rolling around kicking over the Gatorade. I barely hear the knock on the door, but she does and jerks back from my face.

"Caplan?" my mom calls. "Can I come in?"

I'm frozen, but Mina moves quickly, scooping up her clothes and stepping silently through the other door that leads to Ollie's room.

"Caplan?"

"Come in!" I say, and drop down to my knees in front

of the toilet because I can't think of what else to do. She opens the door and sees the shower curtain, crumpled in the tub, and the spilled pool of red Gatorade.

"My god," she says, "did things get violent in here?"

I give a noncommittal grunt and don't take my face out of the toilet. She comes and kneels next to me, pushing the hair off my forehead.

"Oh, you're burning up!"

"I'm fine, Mom."

"Honey, you're all flushed—"

"It's nothing—"

"You feel like you have a fever." She presses her hand to my forehead and then stands to rummage around in the medicine cabinet.

"Mom, I promise I'm okay."

"Take this," she says, handing me Tylenol, "and get into bed, all right?"

"Sure, right."

"Here, I'll—"

"Mom! I've got it!"

I practically shove her from the bathroom. I rest my hand on Ollie's doorknob for one second and then throw myself into his room.

He's sitting on his bed with homework spread around him, staring out his window, with his mouth hanging open. He turns to me and points toward the window.

"Mina," he says, "no clothes, came in, bra, winked at me. Climbed out my window."

I run to the window and look down, but nobody's there.

"Did you guys just—were you just about to—"

"I don't know," I say, trying to make my thoughts go

in a straight line, but her face just pounds in my head, like the bass of a song.

"Then WHY are you standing here talking to me?" He jumps to his feet, and his papers go flying, floating all over the room. "GO! THIS IS IT!"

"THIS IS WHAT?" I don't know why I'm yelling back, but it feels good.

"THIS IS THE MOMENT!"

"FUCK! OKAY!"

I run from his room and down the stairs, past my mom, mid tying her sneakers in the foyer, and out the front door. I cut purposefully across the street, not noticing anything or anyone, with my eyes on Mina's blue front door. I give the brass knocker a good smack. Nothing happens at first, and I feel like my heart is going to explode out of my throat, and then Mina's mother opens the front door.

"Caplan?"

"Gwen! Mrs. Stern! Is . . . is Mina here?"

"Caplan, why aren't you wearing any clothes?"

I look down at my boxers. "Damn."

"Is everything okay?"

"Yes," I say, "I mean, I think so. Sorry I said *damn*. I meant that to be in my head. Actually, I think things might be more than okay?" She's still looking at me blankly, blocking my way, and I feel so wired that I open my mouth and say, "Mina and I just kissed and then my mom walked in so she ran off and so now I'm here to talk to her and I'm only in my boxers cause I got too drunk last night and threw up all over my clothes, not because I was kissing your daughter with no clothes on, that part was just sort of a coincidence."

I wait for her to slam the door in my face. Then with an unreadable expression, she steps aside. I don't wait for her to change her mind. I hurtle up the stairs to Mina's room. The door is open, and she is standing there looking completely normal in her clothes again and making a very similar face with sky-high eyebrows to the one her mother just made when she opened the door to me.

"What the hell!" she whispers.

"I'm sorry!"

"What are you doing here?"

"I don't know!"

"Why didn't you put clothes on?"

"I DON'T KNOW!"

"Shhh!" She claps a hand over my mouth, and we both look toward the door, but some sort of music is drifting up the stairs. She cocks her head, confused, and I can't help but reach out and touch her face.

"Jesus Christ!" She flicks me, and I jump back and fold my hands behind my back.

"Sorry!"

"What did you say to my mom?!"

"I just—I was casual and subtle. I just told her I—that we kissed—"

"Oh my god—"

"And that I wanted to talk to you."

"And what did she say?!"

"Well, nothing, but she let me come up."

"Oh my god," she says again, looking back at the door. The music is even louder now. "What were you thinking, Caplan?"

"Um. Well. That maybe this was a moment? And I didn't—I didn't want to miss it?"

She looks at me hard. "My god," she says, "I can't believe you got a boner—"

"Stop! Stop talking about it or it's gonna happen again!"

This just makes her laugh. She puts her hands over her eyes, and her shoulders shake.

"Mina," I say weakly.

She takes a deep, shaky breath. She drops her hands and looks at me.

"Okay," she says eventually.

"Okay what?"

"That would be okay. If it happened again."

"It would?"

"Yes."

26
Mina

That thing happens again, where my mind goes empty and hums.

"Are you sure you're okay?"

"Yes," I say again, "I'm sure."

"Okay."

Something about his voice makes me pause and look up at him.

"Are you?"

"Yeah," he says. "Yeah, I'm just. I'm nervous?"

I pull on his hand, so he gets on his knees, too. I put our foreheads together.

"It's just me."

He puts his hand in my hair, behind my ear.

"That's the thing. It's you."

After, we lie in my bed together, both out of breath, in a bizarre state of shock.

I'm not going to pretend that I haven't ever thought about this moment before. But all I feel now is immobile with surprise, a total humiliation for whichever one of us will have to break the silence, and absolute dread of what they will say. I think if it's me, I will open my mouth and something massive and irreversible will come out.

When we were growing up, before we were too big for my twin bed, we would sleep head to toe. Whenever I couldn't fall asleep, I would close my eyes and imagine how his face might look, down at the other end of the bed. Long, light lashes, sparse, decisive freckles, the mole under his right eye, the hair right at his temple, so blond in childhood it was almost white. I'd done this since I was so young that it never seemed wrong or romantic. Then one night, when I was twelve years old, in that strange twilight between sleeping and waking with his striped socked feet an inch from my nose, I thought about what it would be like to kiss him. I was so embarrassed, it woke me all the way up, and I went and got sick in the bathroom.

I can feel him looking at me now, but I cannot turn my head. I look at the ceiling, the morning light against the dark molding.

"What is this music?" he asks. We both listen. I try to focus on the words and not the huge thing settling over me, or maybe it is coming from inside of me, clawing its way out, after all these years.

Where has the time all gone to?
Haven't done half the things we want to

"It's my dad's," I say. "He had a big record collection. He loved old musicals."

"I didn't even know you had a record player."

"I can't remember the last time we used it."

"What's this song?" he asks. I'm about to say I have no idea, but then I recognize it.

"Some Other Time."

The lyrics are as clear as if they're playing in the room with us. It must be comically loud for my mom, downstairs.

"Why do you think she put it on? To set the mood?" he asks.

"No, I think just to give us privacy." I sit up and reach for my shirt, try to feel normal, put my feet flat on the floor. "I can't remember the last time there was music in the house," I say, just to say something. I stand, pull on my shorts, and turn around to face him.

He's lying in my bed with his hands behind his head, watching me. When he sees my face, his falls. "What's wrong?"

"Nothing—"

"You should get dressed—"

"I only wore my underwear here." He laughs, and I try to laugh, too, and then I feel like crying. I turn around and find a big T-shirt for him. He watches me carefully as he pulls it over his head.

"Hey," he says, "are you okay?"

It's a Two Docks High Science Olympiad shirt, with a periodic table on the front. Underneath, it says, "WE ARGON TO BARIUM."

"Yes, I'm fine," I say, "but I think you should go."

He looks at me, bewildered. "Go?"

"Yes."

"Right now? After we just—"

"Oh, don't be like that." I turn and pretend I'm going

to make my bed. "You've had sex plenty of times." I feel panicked, like if I'm not alone in the next thirty seconds, I'll explode.

"Not like that."

I keep folding.

"Look, if you want me to go, I'll go, but I think we should figure this out together."

"Figure what out?"

"Will you please look at me?"

I try to.

"This was always going to be hard," he says. "I mean, it was always going to be confusing and different, but if we want it to work, then—"

"What do you mean, if we want it to work?"

"Well," he says, "if we want to, like, be together—"

"Caplan, we can't be together."

"Why?" He is looking at me like he's genuinely confused.

I close my eyes. "Because. You don't see me that way."

"I do!"

"Since when?"

"I don't know, since, well—"

"Since you got jealous of Quinn? Since Hollis dumped you?" *Pick one*, I think. *Pick A, or pick B, turn in your test, and go home.*

"I don't know when it changed, but it changed, okay?"

"But then it could change back! And it doesn't even matter, because we're graduating in six days, and it doesn't make sense to . . . to hold hands and go to prom and then say good-bye."

"We . . . we won't say good-bye," he says slowly. "We'll figure it out."

"And then we'll, what? Start dating? And do long distance?"

"I thought you might go to Michigan?"

"So we'll fall in love and live happily ever after?"

He looks at me for a long time. "Do you not like me, that way?"

When I don't answer, he says, his face stricken, "Did you not—not want to—do you wish we hadn't—"

"No," I say. "No, you asked me like every ten seconds if I was sure."

"I asked you twice."

I go back to the bedsheets. "It doesn't matter if I like you that way or not."

"Mina, if you don't, then just tell me, okay?"

"It's like Quinn said! There's something fucked up about us. It isn't normal."

"What's so bad about that?" he asks. "We're, you know—okay, yeah, maybe it's a little intense or unusual, but—"

"A little intense?" I'm laughing even though I don't find it funny at all. "Caplan, a therapist would have a field day. A little intense—it would be wrong, it would be unhealthy and ill-advised—"

"Ill-advised? Jesus, what's so bad about it?"

"Take your pick!" I yell. "Your daddy issues or mine—"

"Oh, come on—"

"Your savior complex, my intimacy issues—it doesn't matter if it's our fault or not, it's just the way it is."

"BUT WHO CARES!" I'm glad he's yelling and not looking at me the way he was before. "Why do you have to be so smart about everything, all the time, why do you have to analyze it all, none of that matters!"

"Of course it matters! We aren't equals!"

This pulls him up short.

"You can't be with someone," I say, "who isn't your equal."

"How can you even say that? What are you even fucking talking about?"

"I'm alive because of you."

"Mina—come on—that is just—"

"It's true!" I yell at him. "You know it's true. That's why you stayed over so many nights, and you know it—"

"Mina, stop—"

"You slept on my floor for a week in eighth grade, because you knew what I would do if you left. You knew. And no one else was there to stop me but you."

He doesn't say anything, but he doesn't look away, either.

"Admit it," I say. "Don't lie."

"I didn't know for sure. But I—yes, I worried about it. Is that so bad? That I was scared of—that I would have done anything? To keep you here?"

"No. No, it isn't bad. But it isn't love."

"Well, what is it, then?"

"It's obligation."

We look at each other for a long time. His face could turn me inside out.

"What am I supposed to do, then?" he asks. "What am I supposed to do with all my . . . you know. My feelings for you?"

I wish I'd given him any other fucking shirt. He looks too funny. Too real. Too himself, and I feel a sob working its way up my throat.

"You handle it," I say. "I've done it for years."

"Mina, if you feel the way I feel about you—I don't care whether you think it's good or bad. I need you to tell me."

"YOU don't even feel how you think you feel!"

"WHAT DOES THAT MEAN?"

"Taking *care* of someone isn't the same thing as caring about them! You've . . . you've Stockholmed yourself into thinking you have some kind of crush on me when it's—when that's just—"

"It's not a crush." He looks at the wall. "Sometimes I wish you'd just turn your brain off."

"See. There you go. You don't like me. If I did that, then I wouldn't be me."

His face is still turned away. I brace myself for what he'll say next. Then, without looking back, he just leaves. I hear him go down the stairs and out the front door. The music shuts off. I lock my door, in case my mom tries to come talk to me. My hands are shaking. The house is silent again.

Like an obedient and practiced crazy person, I turn on the shower, get in, and wait for the panic attack. But it never comes. I sit down under the water and lean my head against the glass door. I try not to think of how he looked, turned away from me, the set of his jaw, like he was trying not to cry. I press my forehead harder against the glass. How could I have said things to him, to make him look that way? What kind of person am I?

I'm pressing too hard, and the door swings open. Water spatters the bathroom floor. I watch it for a second and then pull myself up. I shut off the shower, use my towel to dry the tile, and get into bed all wet. It isn't us, I think, or our friendship that is so intense, or so heavy, or so wrong. It is me. And whatever kind of person I may be, that is why I had to do it. Because he deserves better.

My mom knocks quietly on my door. I ignore her. Hollis texts me and asks me if I'd like to come to her graduation dinner tomorrow night. She makes clear it is just girls. I realize I don't know the rules. I had sex with her ex-boyfriend. If she knew, maybe she wouldn't invite me, so it wouldn't be fair to go. I reply right away that I have a family obligation, because if I wait to do it, I'll cave. It is this, inexplicably, that finally makes me cry.

In a dizzy circle, my thoughts chase one another. I want to go to Caplan and say sorry, but I cannot take any of it back. And it isn't worth hurting him again, and maybe I won't be able to a second time, but I must be able to, over and over, if I want to be his friend, and then I arrive at the truth at the bottom of it all. We will never be friends again, never in the same way. I close my eyes and try to let my body feel as still and as heavy as possible, so I do not stand up and run to his door.

Quinn texts me and asks if he can come over to talk. I tell him not to worry. My mom texts me from downstairs and asks me what I want to eat for dinner. I tell her I'm not hungry.

Later, when it is dark, and I must have fallen asleep, she knocks.

I forget, in my drowsiness, that I am self-quarantining and open the door.

"Can I come in?" she asks. She's holding a pizza box.

"You look like a deliveryman."

I step aside, and she comes and sets the box right on

the floor. She sits in front of it and waits for me, and I feel too weary to protest so I go and sit, too. She takes out a slice.

"You don't like pizza," I say. "It upsets your stomach."

"That's true." She takes one bite and hands it to me. I eat it slowly and hope she will not ask me about the circus of dramatics that have played out in our house today. The music, the door slamming, the shouting, like a Broadway show. She doesn't say anything, though. She just sits quietly, until she is satisfied that I've eaten two slices. Then she takes the box downstairs, telling me on the way out that the rest will be in the fridge if I'm hungry again later.

I do not exactly feel better, but I am less hollow, and less shaky, and of course, not entirely alone, as I sometimes pretend I am.

At midnight, I go down in the dark for another slice. I pause as I shut the fridge door. There are two new cards stuck there, underneath *Chrysanthemum*. I slip them out of their magnets to look at the backs. In my mother's looping hand, faded, written years ago—*Jane Eyre* and *Anne of Green Gables*. These are the books I wrote my final English paper on. My mom must know this, since she was at the honors award ceremony. The *Anne of Green Gables* card is from the 1980s. The *Jane Eyre* one is from 1923. I take them to the table and inhale two more cold pieces of pizza while familiarizing myself with the list of names. Then I slip back upstairs and root around in my closet until I find what I'm looking for. It's creased and frayed at the edges—a borrowing card from the original Brothers Grimm collection of fairy tales, the last one she gave me before she stopped working. An unnerving, gory bible for a seven-year-old, but I wouldn't put it down, and my mother didn't mind. More than not minding, she understood. She understood more about me than I'd realized, if she saved *Jane Eyre* and *Anne of Green Gables* for me all those years ago, knowing someday I'd read them and someday I'd love them. I take the Brothers Grimm card back down and hang it up with all the others, adding to our little graveyard.

Somehow, though I've spent all day in bed, I manage to fall asleep, drifting off on thoughts of orphans, and bloody heels in golden slippers, and why Cinderella would have run each night from the ball when faced with all she'd ever wished for.

The next morning, I make myself shower again, not to cry this time but to wake up. On and off throughout the night, I thought about the weeks, frankly the months, growing up, when my mother had no idea if or when I was eating. I decide she is trying, and so will I. I brush and braid my hair and dig out a hideous old pair of glasses, to look like myself, because my usual pair are still at Hollis's.

I go downstairs, make coffee and toast, and see a new card on the fridge, a bit apart from the others. I notice right away its number is in the same Dewey decimal group as Jane Eyre: 823.8. English fiction, 1837–1900. The title is *Middlemarch* by George Eliot. I haven't read this one yet and don't know who George Eliot is. I go to the bookshelf in the living room and scour it for ten minutes before realizing the book is already laid out for me on the coffee table. It's been several weeks since I opened something new. I've been meaning to, but have been very busy contending with nonfictional people and all the uncontainable, irreversible mess of knowing them. I don't know what makes me do it, but I take *Middlemarch* with me into my dad's study and turn on the record player. I pick the first thing I touch, without looking at it. Then I start to read.

Eventually, my mom comes and stands in the doorway.

"This song was playing when you were born," she says.

"Really?"

"Your dad brought his Discman to the hospital to distract me."

"What's it called?"

"'La Vie en Rose.'"

I listen to the lyrics for a minute.

"It's not very me, is it?" I say. I mean to be funny, but it comes out too sad.

"You can understand it?"

"I've taken French since ninth grade."

For a moment, I'm afraid she'll cry, but instead she comes and sits next to me on the arm of the big chair. She reads over my shoulder, a bit slower than I do, but I pause before turning each page, to be sure she's ready. Eventually, I let my head rest on her shoulder.

"I owe you an apology," she says suddenly. I realize she's gotten to the end of the chapter before I have. I read to the bottom of the page before answering.

"What for?"

"I didn't want to worry you, or hurt you, more than you were already hurting, so I just . . ."

"Avoided me?"

"I thought I was helping you. By keeping things from you. I don't think I was."

"It's all right," I say. "I kept things from you, too."

She dips her chin at me and waits with her eyebrows raised. I feel so steady and so comfortable with her there next to me, on the arm of his big leather chair. In front of us on the desk is a photo from their wedding, all his school friends, lifting her over their heads like she's crowd-surfing.

"Can I tell you another time?"

"Of course," she says. "I'm not going anywhere." When she stands up to make lunch, I follow her, moving to the couch with my book.

I realize that I've miraculously forgotten, in all my distraction, to read the last page first, as is my tradition whenever I start a new book. I flip ahead.

Later, washing my hands in the kitchen and looking absently out the window, I see Caplan and Quinn walking down the block. They look unlike themselves, and serious, but at least they're not swinging at each other. Caplan is still wearing my periodic table shirt. I move away from the window as they draw closer, and return to the couch, to my mother, fast asleep, and to my book, which is, despite my miserable attitude, excellent.

I'm irritated that the day feels long and lonely to me. This is how I used to spend all my days, and I never minded before.

Just as it is getting dark, someone rings the doorbell. Caplan always uses the knocker. He said in fourth grade that it made him feel like a knight at a castle, but perhaps he is doing this to get me to come to the door. I go warily and peer through the viewer, but it's not Caplan.

It's Quinn. He waves at me. I liked him. I liked that he liked me. Does that mean I liked him? Does everyone else need to ask this question? Shouldn't a person just know it, when they like someone? Whatever it was, it was a flicker. Caplan is a forest fire. I open the door.

"Hey," he says.

"Hi."

"Sorry to just drop by. I was in the neighborhood, and you weren't answering texts."

"That's okay," I say.

"I just, you know, wanted to apologize."

"You don't have to. It's okay."

"Right, but I want to."

"I can't really tell at this point," I say, looking past him at Caplan's house, where thankfully the windows are dark, "whose fault it all is."

Quinn smiles. "Me, neither, I guess."

I try to think of something else to say and end up looking at my feet.

"I also wanted to say—you know, no hard feelings, and in the spirit of that—if you still wanted to go to prom, I would."

"Are you trying to get laid?"

He blinks at me and then explodes into laughter. It takes him a second to come back together. "God, Mina, you're fucking funny."

"Thank you."

"And no, I meant as friends. I'm not an idiot. I've known for a while."

"Known what?"

"Well, after you and Caplan kissed, that night at Ruby's, you didn't kiss me again."

"We kissed after that, I thought—"

"Well, sure," he says, "like I kissed you, and you were nice and kissed me back and stuff, but it's not the same, you know. You can tell when someone is like, *Hell yeah, I want this*, versus, like, *Sure, why not?*" His hands are in his pockets, like it's nothing.

I struggle for a moment, and then I throw my arms around him. "Thanks for knowing that," I say.

He hugs me back. "I think that's, like, the bare minimum, right?"

"Right," I say.

I pull away and try to compose myself.

"So, whaddya say," he says, "prom as friends?" He pulls something out of his pocket—a little bundle of what look like flowers, made of gauzy fabric and tissue paper, in pink and blue and green. They're tied together and bound to a length of ribbon.

"Did you make this?" I ask.

"It's supposed to be a corsage," he says.

It goes without saying, no one has ever brought me flowers. It is not something I ever thought I wanted or cared about, but I suppose lots of people think that, until someone is standing in front of you with them. Even if they're the wrong person.

"That's—that's so—thank you," I say. "But I think it would be best, for everyone, if everything just went back to normal. Plus, I never even got a dress."

He smiles a little sadly and looks down at the corsage.

"And you keep that. Give it to someone else. You deserve your hell-yeah."

He nods. "All right. Fair point. So do you."

"Wait," I say, suddenly remembering, "stay right

here." I run up to my bedroom and return with my hands behind my back. "I got you something, too, and it really wouldn't be right to give it to anyone else or for you to go to prom without it."

I hold out the little red ball in one hand.

"Is that—"

"It's a clown nose."

He stares at it and then looks up at me.

"Mina," he says, "you may be weird, but you have a really cool way of doing things."

He leaves then, loping toward his skateboard that he's left on my lawn. He rattles down the walk and does a little jump over the curb, off into the twilight, with the nose in one hand and the flowers in the other.

Monday is Senior Skip Day, which works just fine for me. I try not to look online—a bad habit I've developed since Hollis posted the picture of me and made me an Instagram account—at the posts of everyone at Little Bend. There are videos of them swinging on the rope with its big knot at the bottom and jumping in. It's tied to the highest branch of a maple on the banks, reaching out over the river where it curves and runs the deepest. They lie out on the banks and cheer for each other when someone swings particularly high or lets go of the rope at the top of its arc. I don't see Caplan, but I'm positive he's there. Especially if he and Quinn have made up. In one video, Hollis climbs the rope like she's in gym class, all the way to the top, where it meets the maple. Then, she lets herself drop, slicing toward the water from that impossible height. I tell myself I would hate being there, all things considered. I'd never jump. Not in a million years.

I know next they will go to Pond Lake. It's customary for the seniors, the fun tradition-oriented ones, to stand together in a line on the dock that faces west, into the sunset, and dive off and race to the dock on the other side. I used to go and watch them with Caplan and our moms when we were young. It's the sort of thing the whole town comes out to see. I decided somewhere around middle school that it was cheesy and stopped going. Still, I watch the sun's progress across the sky, make up chores for myself, and try not to think of the one year I can remember best: on my father's shoulders with a sparkler in my hand, watching the teenagers who seemed so grown up to me then. They tossed themselves out, dark against the pink blaze of the sky, into the flickering water, that space between, impossibly vast to me.

Just as I am settling in for the day to feel peacefully bored and sorry for myself, the house phone rings, strident and jarring. No one ever calls our house phone, except for my grandparents. I sit in my chair at the table, where I have been pretending to read and actually looking at all my classmates' Instagram accounts like a freak, and glare at the phone on the wall as it rings and rings.

Without forming any sort of plan, I stand up so fast I knock over the chair and pick up.

"Hello, Nana. Yes, I'm well. Actually, I'm excellent. I've decided I will not be going to Yale next fall. Yes. Yes,

I know that. No. Actually, I am listening. I'm just not changing my mind."

She asks to speak to my mother.

"Of course. Just a moment."

I carry the phone with me up the stairs and enter her room without knocking. She's lying in bed, on her computer. I hold out the phone.

"Who is it?"

"Who else would it be?" I say. "I've told her I'm not going to Yale. Now she wants to talk to you."

My mother looks at the phone for a long time. I can sense my grandmother growing irritated, miles away, but I do not care. I don't care about anything except my mom, taking over, taking the phone, being in charge. She moves the covers aside like she's in a dream, stands up, and walks past me. I stand there, still holding out the phone, sure she'll return. Then I hear the front door open and close. I hang up.

I try to convince myself that this was a win. I decided, and I told them, and I didn't need any help. I didn't need anyone else.

Then I get into her bed, where I haven't been since I was a child, and sob. I was convinced I'd cried as much as one human girl can possibly cry in one lifetime, but this time, I outdo myself. I really go for it. It is almost impressive. I yell and weep into the pillows, and ruin the silk sheets, and kick the phone off the bed, and promise myself, swear, that I will never put my head on her shoulder again.

My phone rings in my pocket, and I pull it out to turn it off, but then I see a missed call and several texts from Caplan.

hi

i know we're not talking right now and you obviously want space from me and I'm trying to do that

but your mom just walked into our house like

freaking out

and I wanted to make sure everything is okay and if you need someone we can pause, again

ignore these texts, if not

all right they're going into my mom's room and they're talking about you so I'm gonna eavesdrop because that's what I'd want you to do for me

if you don't wanna know, stop reading now

wait

it's about yale

they're calling your grandparents

omg

ur mom just told them you're not going

she says it's ur decision and that you need a fresh start

holy shit

she just said

"frances, i don't give a fuck what you think"

is frances grandma or grandpa

sorry doesn't matter

all right that's all

i hope it's okay i texted you

i bet whatever you did to make this happen it was awesome

rock on

i miss you

I start to type and then delete so many different things. Each one is too much and then not enough. In the end, I say thank you for the space, and thank you for telling me. Almost immediately, he responds.

> do you want to go to the dock jump?
> i know it's not your thing but asking just in case

I stand and slowly reverse the wreckage of my meltdown, to put off responding. I place the house phone on the nightstand, retrieve the pillows from the floor, and remake the bed. Her laptop has also slipped off onto the carpet and sits open on the ground. When I pick it up, the screen comes to life. I can't help but read the email's subject line. Someone wants to open a children's library in East Lansing. The screen of the computer glows at me, a window into the museum of another life, where a distant little sister of myself in a far-off universe used to live. I would lie between my parents in bed in the mornings, and we'd quiz each other on the Dewey decimal call numbers: 398.2 for my fairy tales; 741.5 for my dad's comics; 823.7—my mom's favorite, all the Jane Austen; 567.9 for books about dinosaurs. I couldn't tell you why I remember that one.

Then my mom would say, *They need me at a library in Oklahoma, Arizona, California,* and my dad and I would say, *No, too far, don't go,* but we were only joking, and she knew it. I'd say, *Come home with stories,* and she always did.

Once the room is in order and the bed is tight and fresh again, I look at it for a moment, and then I climb back in. I lie there until my mom comes home.

She crawls in next to me.

"It's all taken care of now," she says. "Don't worry."

"Thank you," I say.

"I'm sorry I left."

"That's all right," I say. "Sometimes you need a friend to hit Send."

We lie together in her bed for a few minutes.

"Will we be okay with money?" I ask eventually.

"Oh, I think so," she says. "I don't know if you've noticed, you and I don't really get out much."

I laugh into my hands, under my cheek.

Then she says, "I've been thinking about working again. There's a new children's library opening."

"I know," I say. "I snooped. Your computer was open."

"Well," she says, "they're also looking for a new librarian, for the public schools in Two Docks."

"That's interesting," I say.

"I thought so, too."

We are quiet then. Our breathing syncs up.

Eventually, she says, "I don't want you to worry about money. The house is ours. Not much they can do about that."

"It is?" I ask. I run my fingers along the thin perfect line of stitches on the pillowcase.

"Oh yes. Your dad made sure of that early on. Aaron was a planner and a worrier, like you. A bit of a doomsdayer, honestly."

My fingers go still. I cannot remember her ever telling me something like this.

"I guess it's not really fair to tease him now. When he can't defend himself."

"I don't think he'd mind," I say.

I can't quite see her face, in the dimmed blackout-curtained world of her room, half hidden under the blanket. I think she is smiling.

She says, "So what are you thinking you'll do?"

"About Caplan?"

"About college. Where will you go? Michigan?"

"Oh," I say. "Right. I don't know yet."

"Well, I can't wait to see."

To my surprise, I find myself saying, "Me, too."

We fall asleep there, just like that, at 5:00 p.m., and that is my Senior Skip Day.

27
Caplan

The best thing about Michigan summers is that as soon as it hits June, the sun doesn't go down until after nine. The days go on forever. That's how it feels.

Bearing this in mind, it's pathetic that I miss the jump because I'm waiting for Mina to text me back. I don't really mean to. I just hang around my front steps for over an hour, acting like I'll leave any second, hoping she'll come out at the last minute, and then all at once it's dusk, and I know it's already happened. That's what I get, for ignoring the sky and letting the sun rise and set with her.

My mom gets home at 10:00.

"You didn't have to wait for me to eat," she says while I set the table for us. I shrug. "How was the jump?"

"Oh, I didn't end up going."

"Really?"

"I'm not in the mood."

"To jump? To talk about it?" When I don't answer, she says, "To graduate?"

"Will it hurt your feelings if I eat in my room?"

"Yes, but I get it. Where's Ollie?"

"He walked over to the lake to watch with his friends. They're at the diner now. Want me to pick him up?"

"Eat first," she says.

At midnight, I feel more awake than I've ever felt. I don't want to admit it, but I care about the dock jump. I care a lot. I've never missed one. And now I've missed my own. I can't stop feeling angry at Mina, even though it isn't her fault I stood around waiting for her. Then I just feel angry at myself. The idea of bad omens takes root in my brain and works its way down into my feet, and I start pacing. If I don't jump, if I'm someone who sat and waited and missed it, I'll always be someone who sits and waits, and I'll never move on, I'll spend the rest of my loser life stuck thinking about how I peaked in high school, thinking about Mina, thinking about those two docks, and everyone else jumping in, moving forward, crossing that in-between without me.

I go down to the kitchen and write a note for Ollie in case he wakes up. My mom is already back at the clinic with the car, so I slip out the back door and set off on foot to the lake.

When I get there, the water looks black and creepy. I walk out to the middle of the west dock, take off my socks and shoes, and try not to think about fish. Are there fish in the lake? I've never noticed. I take my shirt off. I stick my toe in. It's colder than I thought it would be. I guess it's barely summer yet. This is stupid. I don't know what I'm doing here.

I look up at the other dock and try to judge the distance. Then I see her. She's sitting on the edge, in a white

T-shirt that catches the moon. It's too dark to make out her face, but I know her posture. I know the shape of her knee, sticking up, under her chin. I stand, and she sits, and we look at each other. I want to call out, but I don't want to interrupt whatever is between us. It feels so quiet and still, like a dream. I stay as long as I can, waiting for her to call to me, to do something, and then I can't wait any longer.

I dive in. The water is cool, but the shock is good, and I go a fair distance before needing to breathe. Then, I swim. It's farther than I thought, but I don't pause to clock my progress. I just keep pushing forward. This is better, I think, in the silent gloom beneath the water. This means more than jumping with everyone else, at sunset. This is meant to be. This is just for us. I pull my arm out of the water one more time and reach the worn wood with my fingertips. I pull myself up and look left, then right, shivering. But she's gone.

On Tuesday morning, I wake up with sticky lake hair, so I know at least I was there last night. I make Ollie's bed and then get back into my own. Some hours later, my mom comes to my door.

"Skip Day was yesterday," she says.

"I think I'm sick," I say.

"With what?"

I look at her, sizing up the pros and cons of telling the truth. Then, outside, a car horn blares. There is only one car and one person capable of that sound. It goes on and on and on. I finally get up and move past my mom and go outside, where Hollis is parked in front of my house in her white tank of a car. The windows are painted for Spirit Day. The horn stops. She rolls down the window.

"What are you doing, Hollis?"

"Picking you up. Let's go. It's almost lunch."

"I'm not going to school today," I say. She leans on the horn again. "Holy shit, what is your problem?"

"It's, like, your last real day of school ever," she says, "and I get it, you're moping."

"I am not—"

"But guess what? My long-term first-ever boyfriend and I recently broke up, and I'm in the mood to mope, too, but I'm not, because this time matters, and there isn't much of it left." She has two green stripes under her eyes like a football player, and she looks ready to run me over.

"Hollis, look."

"They're giving out yearbooks today, and I deserve to have you sign mine after everything."

"Hollis—"

"I've mourned and let go of my daydreams—*years* in the making, by the way—of holding hands for the dock jump, and dancing at prom, but I'm not giving up this. So pull yourself together and get in the car."

"I have to get dressed."

"I have all your clothes that I need to return in my trunk."

She pops it. Folded neatly on top of a pile in a brown paper bag are my favorite shorts she used to sleep in, and my TDHS track shirt.

We don't talk in the car, but she plays music and rolls the windows down. The air feels good. I realize that, besides my walk with Quinn, I've barely been outside in daylight since the party.

We get to school just after lunch starts, and I shove off the déjà vu of walking from the parking lot with Hollis after getting dressed in her trunk.

I pause when I see the table in the distance, the best one, under the trees, where all our friends are spraying each other with green silly string and taking still, somehow, more photos.

"She's not there," Hollis says. "I don't know where she's eating. She isn't answering my texts."

"Don't take it personally," I say.

When we reach everyone, people cheer for me like I've come home after being away a long time. I only missed one day, I think, like a piece of shit. Then I try to remember the last time I went a single day without seeing at least one of them, and I can't. Quinn gives me a beard with the silly string, and even though it's fucking annoying of him, I know it means we're good. When he came over on Sunday, I went first and said sorry, since he was the one who asked to talk, and that's harder to do in some ways. I might not have. We went through everything and also went a bunch of blocks without saying anything. The parts that stuck out to me most were when he said it isn't my fault but sometimes it's really hard to be my friend and when he asked if I'm okay.

Ruby hands me my yearbook, and I throw it into the signing rotation. It's difficult not to get into the spirit. I guess that is the point of the day. I'm flipping through someone's, and I'm thrown off by how many photos there are of me and my friends. I'm sure everyone is represented somewhere, at least once, and our class isn't that big, but an uneven number of the candid shots are of us, varying versions of the same core group. People must hate us, I think. We're those assholes. We invented cliquey. I sign Becca's yearbook with something generic, and when I hand it back to her, she throws her arms around me. She's been crying for days now, every time the subject of graduation comes up.

"You guys are, like, more my family than my family," she says, weeping into my shoulder. I hug her tight, cause she's not wrong. I want to stop the clocks, and run it back, and do everything again differently. Or maybe, if given the chance, I'd just do it all again the exact same way, cause we all just are who we are, but then at least I'd know while it was happening how much it mattered. Or I'd just pause, until I could figure out how to enjoy this day, since I'm going to miss it. How could I not? You can't get used to something and then not miss it. Like the music in the background. White noise. You don't notice it's on, but you notice it's off.

I turn to Hollis. "Thanks," I say.

"You're welcome," she says.

We trade yearbooks. I can only find a tiny bit of space, in the bottom-left corner of the last signing page. I write—

u were high school to me

I think more, and then I add—

and I really loved high school.—Cap

As the period ends, I think I may as well finish out the day now that I'm there, but this is a huge mistake. After the first corner I turn, I see her, in her middle-school glasses, holding her own yearbook to her chest, watching her feet. I stop walking. I wait, like an idiot, for her to look up at me, but she doesn't. It takes more than one person banging into me to get me moving again.

Maybe she didn't see me, I think. Maybe she didn't see me last night, either. Maybe I thought she was looking at me, maybe I felt it, but if I couldn't see her face, how could she see mine? Maybe she wasn't even there. Maybe it was a dream. Maybe I'm losing my mind.

And then the dam cracks and all the hope I'd tried to put to bed lights up in my stomach and the merry-go-round of nauseating bullshit I've ridden to death in my mind cranks to life. In the time it takes to get to class, I've run through everything she said in her bedroom again, making sure I still have it memorized, begging to make it make more sense the hundredth time through. She said we weren't even. Because I took care of her. *But I need you*, I think. I need you, too. I need you more. I'm sure I need you more. It's impossible that anyone could want to see another person's face more than I want to see yours, right now. If it is, I swear to god I hope I never feel it.

I sit in class like a zombie. As far as I can tell, nothing's going on. People sit on top of their desks and keep signing yearbooks. I take mine out for something to do, and it opens to the center fold in my lap. On the left side, there are pictures of everyone from College T-Shirt Day, back in May. There we all are, at the lunch table, a block of primary-colored midwestern schools and Hollis in her NYU purple. In silver script, across the top of the page, it says, *Make new friends*.

On the right, across the bottom of the page in gold, it says, *But keep the old*. None of the photos are posed, and there is something really classic and good about each one, something they've done in the editing to make them look older than they are. I think of all the times I've rolled my eyes at Ruby, always shoving her camera in my face, and decide to thank her when I get the chance. Then, I see us, at the bottom of the page, big and centered, but almost covered by the words *keep the old*. Me and Mina, sitting in the library. She's looking at her book, but she's laughing, and I'm leaning back in my chair, talking with my hands.

People start to move to the next class all around me, and I make myself get up. I accept high fives and act normal, but won't let anyone else sign my yearbook. I am afraid to let go of it or set it down.

Before last period, I see her again out of the corner of my eye at the other end of the main entryway, leaning against one of the big green pillars. She's wearing her dad's blue oxford and shorts. The idea of ignoring each other is so bad that halfway across, I turn right and go out the front doors. I walk around the outside of the school, toward the side door, which will put me quite a walk from my next class.

This is the lowest I've ever been, I think, picking through the hedge, staying close to the building so no one looks out the window and sees me. I'm considering giving up and going home, when I see the door in the distance, propped open. I'd been planning to just bang on it and pray.

Quinn's holding it for me.

"Pathetic," he says, but he steps aside to let me in.

We walk to last period, and the halls are oddly still and empty. Eventually, I can't take the quiet.

"Aren't you gonna tell me to man up?"

"Nah," he says. "You're the golden boy. You're gonna do whatever you want either way."

When I get home, I let myself in and drop my bag on the ground and then remember to pick it up and put it on the bench, like I've done every single afternoon of my life. Like everything is normal. Like it'll never change. I walk into the kitchen and see the rental tux hung on the back of the closet door. Behind it is a second hanger, a new white shirt for graduation. When my mom gets home from work, I'm still sitting there, looking at them.

"If you're skipping this, too," she says, "you're gonna tell me why."

"You got me a new white shirt," I say.

"Well, the other one was bloody. A bad omen for prom. Very *Carrie*-esque. Sorry, you probably don't know that reference—"

"Freaky girl, magic powers," I say. "Yeah. Mina mentioned it once."

She sits next to me, and we look at the tux.

Ollie wanders through the kitchen. "Everyone in my grade thinks you'll be prom king," he says, taking the milk out of the fridge.

I sigh.

"Oh, it must be so hard to be you," my mom says, patting my head.

"And there's a bet going around that if Hollis wins queen, she'll dump a drink on you."

"See? See why I shouldn't go?"

My mom shoos Ollie from the kitchen and comes and sits on the stool next to mine again. She looks at me expectantly.

"If I tell you why, I don't have to go?"

"What if you tell me why and then you do go?"

"Well, I haven't told you what's wrong yet, so how do you know I should go?"

She shrugs. "Senior prom only happens once. Mine sucked, but I'm glad I went."

"Why?"

"Well, if I hadn't, I'd always have to wonder if maybe it would have been wonderful."

I consider this for a second.

"That's my first piece of life advice. It is worse to regret the things you didn't do than the things you did."

"That's such bullshit."

"It's not. I stand by it."

"You don't regret marrying my dad?"

She thinks for a long time. I can't tell if I said it because I want the conversation to end, or because I've been thinking about him more than usual, after what Mina said about our issues, how they may not be our fault, but that doesn't make them less real. I think I've spent my whole life expertly not thinking about anything hard. Then this thing, this stupid thing with Mina slipped through, and the rest came tidal-waving after. I can't remember ever being upset about something for more than two hours, and now I've been walking around, moping, just like Hollis said. Moping and missing shit and taking detours and jumping too late and swimming too slow.

"I'm sorry he didn't come to your graduation party," she says at last.

"It's fine—"

"And no. I don't regret marrying him."

I don't believe her. I look at her.

"Because I got you."

I blink hard.

She puts an arm around me. "My second piece of life advice—"

"Mom—"

"If things aren't right and you need to fix it, it doesn't hurt to dress your best."

"Is that from Pinterest?"

"No. From my brain."

"Fine. Is there a third?"

She thinks.

"If Hollis does win and wants to dump a drink on you tomorrow night, she deserves the chance."

Everyone meets on the school's front lawn to take photos. It's funny, but after all the political dealings of who will take who, there are very few photos where people stand in couples. Mostly it's all the girls posing together, in critical varying groups of twos and threes, while boys loiter around tugging their collars. Then there's a series of disastrous group photos where I guarantee in every single one, someone's eyes are closed, someone's flipping off the camera, or someone is yelling, "Okay, this is it! Everyone look good on three!" During the classic prom pose, Quinn's off to the side with me. We climb up onto the Two Docks High sign and have thirty seconds to get the shot, squatting and doing stupid shit with our hands, before we get yelled at to come down. Because Hollis is also going stag, she takes a photo with all the boys, even me. Then everyone takes photos with their parents.

My mom's at work, but I took a photo with her before leaving the house. She was going on about how she didn't want to take one in her scrubs, but I could tell she was happy after we did it. That was the only picture that mattered to me, so I feel pleasantly disconnected while everyone around me seems uncomfortable and tense.

"I can't believe this whole parade isn't even the prom," Quinn says. "We still have the thing itself."

Prom is at a dumb ballroom with ugly carpet in a hotel off the highway. I have to admit it feels cool to stomp up the fancy steps into the room in all our rented finery, though. Inside, a bunch of circle tables surround the dance floor. It shimmers with colored lights and cheap disco balls, at odds with the rest of the room. I'm hovering on the edge when they announce prom king and queen. Hollis is over by the punch, blinking in the lights and beaming like a movie star.

When they say my name, Quinn and Noah pants me.

Usually, the prom royalty have a dance, and I'm assuming this will be an awkward moment and Hollis will play it off for us and do something charming, like give me the finger, but instead, after they give us our crowns and the music starts, she offers me her arm.

"This is big of you," I say as we revolve on the spot. "There was a bet that you'd dump punch on me."

"Oh, I know. No one gets to predict me."

That's when I realize the song's changed. It's that Taylor Swift one, *We are never ever ever getting back together. Ever.*

"No one ever can," I say. "Who'd you pay to make this happen?"

"No one," she says. "I just asked nicely."

"Well, Quinn predicted you."

"He did not—"

"He did. He bet me days ago we'd dance at prom. He said he'd go pantless under his grad robe if we didn't."

"God, if I'd known that, I'd have just flipped you off and been done with it."

"Well, I'm glad we're having a last dance. You look great," I say, because she does. She's wearing some sort of two-piece situation. A silver strapless thing and a long matching skirt.

She adjusts my crown and smirks. "I used to think it was so unfair that every time we'd break up, I had to see your stupid face the next day. It's gonna be really weird, not having that struggle."

"I'm gonna miss you, too, Hollis," I say.

"Maybe it'll be nice to miss each other. Maybe we'll move on."

"Yeah. Maybe we can be friends."

She rests her head on my shoulder. "We always were friends, Caplan. You just didn't realize."

We're still slow dancing, even though the song is fast and everyone else is jumping up and down around us. One other couple is still locked in a close embrace. I do a double take.

"Is that Ruby? And . . . and Lorraine? Mina's friend Lorraine?"

Hollis glances over her shoulder. "Oh yes. They've been hooking up all year."

"How'd they even meet?" I ask.

"They're both on yearbook. That's why it was so important for Noah to ask Becca. To make sure he didn't ask Ruby. And I didn't want to push her or tell you guys, obviously. I just wanted to leave their way clear."

"Hollis . . ."

"What?"

"I don't know anyone who's a better friend than you."

"Thank you," she says. Then she sighs. "You don't even know the half of it."

"What do you mean?"

"Where's Mina?"

"I don't know," I say. "At home, I guess. She always said she never wanted to go to prom."

"Caplan, you have to let people grow up. People get to change their minds. Whatever. It's fine. As long as you told her you love her."

"*Love* is, like—that's a big word, you know? I didn't want to freak her out."

"You just didn't want to freak yourself out."

"What's that supposed to mean?"

"I dumped you to give you the chance to follow your stupid heart. And you didn't even do it right?"

"Yeah, I mean, we hooked up, and then I pretty much told her."

She just glares some more.

"I basically told her. Like, it was obvious."

Hollis shakes her head. "Wow. All right. I must be a really, really good person or something. Let's go."

She takes my hand and leads me toward the exit.

Quinn catches up to us just before we get to the bottom of those endless grand stairs.

"Are you guys going to get her?" he asks.

"We're going to try," Hollis says.

"Hang on. I have something that'll help."

28

Mina

There's an irrelevant half day of school the day of senior prom. The people who do show up wear face masks and pj's and stuff. I go, to maintain my attendance, and then no one even takes attendance, so I leave after first period.

When I get home, my mom is on the couch.

"Big plans tonight?"

"Nope," I say, flopping next to her. "What are we watching?"

"Let's watch all the movies we can think of with proms in them."

"Are you joking?"

"I can be?"

It's not like I won't be thinking about it, anyway, so I say yes.

By 8:00 p.m., I'm in boxers and a T-shirt I got in elementary school for winning the spelling bee. I get into bed and do my best to feel tired and not pathetic. It doesn't work. My room feels stuffy, so I open the window, and then I end up just sitting and looking out of it. This starts to feel really gratuitous, and so I climb out onto the roof. I've never been out here without Caplan, even though it's my roof and my window, and the thought irritates me so much I forget to feel sad. Suddenly, I am furious with myself, and my life, and every choice I've made to land myself here.

Because if I were a different kind of person, it wouldn't have mattered that I have no date and no friends. I'd throw on some quirky surprising dress and march into the fugly glittery room with my head held high and everyone would be impressed with my pluck. Or if my best friend—let's be honest, my only friend—hadn't been a boy I was always a little in love with, if my tiny narrow life could actually for god's sake at least not be an argument for good old-fashioned sexism, or if I were a normal person with girl-friends, or even one girl best friend, I'd be able to walk in arm in arm with her and overrule the whole ridiculous patriarchal heteronormative notion of a romantic happy ending at eighteen years old. I think about Caplan asking me why I have to analyze everything to pieces, and I actually yell out in frustration. But the street is deserted, and anyone who I wouldn't want to hear me is at prom, being normal.

Then a beam comes sweeping around the corner, lighting up the world. I stay still on my roof in the dark, but when the car pulls into my driveway, I am not all that surprised. It's a cul-de-sac, after all.

He slams the door and comes over to the jungle gym to climb up, and then he sees me.

"Oh," he says, "hi."

I don't say anything, because I'm worried if I do, I'll cry. His crown's slipped off to one side, sitting tilted. He looks better than any boy in any movie.

"Okay," he says. He puts his hands into his pockets and then takes them back out again. "All right. So I came here because I have some stuff I want to say."

I manage to nod.

"So. What I have to say—and you're better at arguing than I am, so I need you to wait till I'm totally finished before you respond, okay—what I have to say is that you said, the other day in your room, that you're alive because of me and that's too much pressure or power or whatever it was, but I am who I am because of you. Which I'd argue is just as big a deal. Every decent thing about me is from knowing you. I've wanted to be just like you, to deserve to be around you, since I was eight. And I don't want to meet whoever I'd be today if that hadn't happened. I don't know myself without you, I don't want to, and I've looked up to you my whole life. And if that means we aren't equals, then fine."

He pauses and takes a deep breath. When I still don't say anything, he plows on.

"The best parts of myself, I got from you, okay? And that, that has to count. For some kind of love."

"Of course it counts—"

"AND—I'm not done—AND I know it's hard to believe because of how shitty I've been and how selfish I've acted and I don't really have a good excuse. The best one I can come up with is that after, you know, caring about you—I mean, loving you—in such an easy way it was basically like . . . like breathing, for so long, well, then falling in love with you just, like, knocked the wind out of me. It was such a different feeling. It's like—like having to learn to breathe again or something, and I got confused because—because I don't know why. Because I was scared. Because I didn't know how you felt."

"Caplan—"

"BUT I've realized—sorry, I'm almost done—I've realized it made me a bad friend. And obviously I don't know jack about love, but I'm pretty sure it's not supposed to do that, so I think I was loving wrong. Probably, because I was doing it without you, and as we already know, I'm no good without you. So. No matter how you feel about me, even if you love me as a friend, or, you know—either way, I'm not gonna let you down ever again. If you, ah, if you decide to let me be your friend. Again." He looks up at me, his chest rising and falling like he's climbing a mountain. "Do you think we could. Be friends again?"

"I don't know how we can."

"I'll do whatever it takes," he says.

"No, it's not you, it's me." I take a deep breath and shove the words out. "I don't see you as just a friend. I don't know that I ever did. Maybe that's why I didn't feel equal, growing up. All the other stuff—"

"But—but, Mina!"

"Stop. Stop smiling like that. It's not a good thing."

"Okay, sorry." He's still smiling so big, his face looks like it's about to split open and set the night ablaze.

"I tried for years. I tried really hard to make it go away," I say.

"I think—I think it's a miracle, if you feel how I feel." Something bursts open, unfolding in my chest, stretching and spreading and filling me up. I feel it everywhere. I feel it in my littlest finger.

"Everything would change. And we have no idea how."

"Mina, you said it yourself, you told me weeks ago, the day I got into college and I asked you to promise me nothing would change. Do you remember what you said?"

"All I can remember about that day is that you got in."

"You promised me, something like, if things have to change, and they do, because they always will, it'll be for something better."

His joy is contagious. It is too much. "Did you get smarter than I am?"

"No, no, I've been thinking this through for days. Just trying to keep up with your brain." He beams up at me, for all the world like we're just hanging out.

"I'm just—I'm overwhelmed. By it," I say finally.

"By what?"

"By who you are. And how I feel."

"Okay. Well, it doesn't have to be this huge thing. We'll take it a step at a time. If you still need space, I'll give you some. If you want to go to prom as friends, we'll go. If you want me to wait here while you think, then I will. We've got all night."

He sits down in the grass. I know right then that even if I went inside and shut the window and went to bed, he'd still be there when I woke up.

A car horn blares.

"Okay, maybe we don't have all night," he says.

I stare at the car, the windshield impossible to see through in the glare of the headlights. Something slides into place. Caplan got out of the wrong side.

"Who drove you here?"

"We couldn't do prom without you."

"We?" And finally, I cry.

"No matter what you feel about me," he says, "I think you should come with us. Or she'll never forgive me." Then he puts his hand into his jacket pocket and pulls out a very familiar corsage. "Plus, Quinn's a sucker for a happy ending."

He reaches up and ties the ribbon around my ankle carefully. Then he just holds my ankle, hanging on, in no rush. I realize I'm smiling now, too. I can't stop.

"So what's next, Mina?"

I wiggle my toes.

"Your call. No wrong answers. Gut instinct."

"I'll come," I say. "I'll come to prom, and we'll take it from there. Now let go."

"Why?"

"So I can go inside and come down."

"But I don't want to let go."

"I'll be quick. I'm just going to use the stairs. I can't climb down out here like you."

"Okay," he says. "Be fast." He stays holding my ankle for another moment, looking at me, all lit up, and then, just as he loosens his grip, I jump. His arm is still raised high, ready to catch me.

Prom

We walk in just in time for the last dance. Hollis wears my spelling-bee shirt, knotted up above her silver skirt, like a pop star. I have on the shimmering top half of her dress, my shorts, Caplan's black jacket, and his crown. He walks in just after us. It's a dramatically late entrance, and everyone turns and stares. I know Hollis is chin up beside me, so I do the same. When I see Quinn, he takes his red nose out of his pocket and puts it on. I stick out my foot so he sees the corsage. He starts to slow clap. Everyone else joins in. It's so loud and lasts so long that I don't remember the only song that played while I was at prom.

Grad

After we've all crossed the stage one by one, Mina and I both stand to present senior speaker remarks, which, this year, is our video. As it plays, we stay onstage, but off to the side. We get to watch everyone's faces change when they hear their own name. Jim Ferraby, Mina's square dancing partner from eighth grade, tells his best friend he's in love with her and hopes he's told her in person by now, and I want to laugh at how big my own feelings are to me, and how obvious and unoriginal they are when you zoom out, even in my tiny hometown. Lorraine tells Ruby she wishes she could do with words what Ruby does with a camera. She thanks Ruby for seeing her. Jamie Garrity thanks me for always holding the side door. At some point, I don't remember deciding to, but I take Mina's hand. I keep it close between us, folded in our robes so no one can see, just in case she'd be embarrassed.

·   ·   ·

When Quinn's face fills the screen, he says that Hollis is every human person's dream girl, and then he says, "Nah, nah, retake that, I can't say that," and it gets a standing ovation.

(Later that night, I hear from him, and Mina hears from her: He confessed to Hollis at the big grad party at Noah's lake house that he's actually never had full sex, technically, to completion, and he really doesn't want to go to college a virgin. So they do it in the parents' master bathroom, right in the tub, and then they take a bath together and make a giant mess. Quinn told Hollis it was the greatest night of his life, and she laughed so hard she got water up her nose. She told him she didn't know about the greatest night of her life, but that it was actually probably the best sex she'd ever had.)

When people stand for Quinn's video, Hollis stands, too, and takes a bow.

Then there is Mina, looking everywhere but the camera, elusive as always, saying that I am everyone's favorite person. And there's me, saying that she is mine. For one second, my stomach drops, to see my face so huge, open, and saying something I didn't even know was so true at the time, but I look down at Mina, and she is making the same face for me. I put our hands up in the air together, and everyone absolutely loses it. Then she gets this gleam in her eye. She's looking at me and shaking her head like she can't believe something, and then she kisses me, right onstage, in front of everyone. If graduation had been inside, the roof would have blown. The sound hits the stratosphere. Birds take off. Quinn is standing on his chair, wolf whistling and giving us both his middle fingers. A teacher has to pull him down, but there isn't much else they can do. They've already given him a diploma.

We let our moms take the cars, and we walk home holding hands. I don't think we've let go once since we started. People cheer for us as we pass by, friends and strangers; it's graduation day, and everyone is out on their porches to see the seniors on their way.

When we get to Corey Street, it's quiet. I tell her I love her again. She tells me she's taking a gap year and moving to New York. She is going to leave with Hollis to drive east as soon as next week, but she doesn't drop my hand while she says it. She tells me that if she stays for the summer, like this, with me, she will not be able to say good-bye. She will follow me to Michigan, and then everywhere, for the rest of her life. I want for one second to get down on my knees and beg her to do exactly that. Instead, I put my hand up to my face, because the sun is setting and bouncing off the houses' windows into my eyes, and I hum a bit of "Some Other Time."

·   ·   ·

She tells me she missed her dad today. She says she wishes he could know how she turned out, what she decided, and where she's going and not going. I tell her he would have been proud of her. I tell her he is proud of her. And then, because I want her to laugh and not cry, I tell her if she's leaving in a week or less, we have to have sex one hundred times before then.

Neither of our families are home yet, so we go up to my room and do it one and a half times, and then we start to fall asleep with all the windows open, because for one more day, we have nothing else to do. She is quiet, breathing on my chest, and I want to stop time, but the sun keeps setting. A slant of golden light slides down my bedroom wall. The room goes dark.

"You never fall asleep with the sun," I say into her hair. She smiles like she's already dreaming. "I don't need you to give me the summer or the rest of our lives, but thank you for this, right now."

She says my name.

She tells me she loves me for the first time.

ON TURNING THE PAGE
BY MINA STERN

In fourth grade, I taught my best friend to read. I know this is factually true, but when he brings it up today and phrases it like this, I'm defensive.

He was not my friend before we started reading together. Actually, he was my enemy, because he was socially and athletically gifted, and I liked to read. It was elementary school, and the rules of that society, in case you've forgotten, are not exactly subtle. Our teacher, in a move that was perhaps ill-advised, set us up as reading partners and effectively asked one eight-year-old to tutor another. This should have been a disaster, but it worked out, if only because of my friend's inherent unflinching curiosity, which was stronger even than his pride or his prejudice (forgive me).

I have been a chronic re-reader since I first learned how. If it had been left up to me, I'm sure I would have read Chrysanthemum *again and again and never moved on. To this day, I will always reach for something I've already read over something new. I understand how little sense this makes—since each and every book I've come to love as a permanent companion was, at one point, brand-new and unknown to me. I used to religiously read the final page of a book before beginning it. I am trying now to stop doing this (since you can flip ahead all you like but you will never be able to change the ending). All the same, that is how unpleasant the unknown is to me, and how critical it is to avoid anything I cannot predict or control.*

The situation of being alive, then, poses a problem for me and has often felt uncomfortable, at times almost impossible. I have no idea where I will end up next year, and the question overwhelms me so much I cannot begin to imagine myself anywhere, much less want myself anywhere.

I think this is why it is important to love people who are different from us and why some of life's terrible inexplicable randomness does have a point, after all, or at least a silver lining. A book you might not think to choose cannot actually leap off the shelf at you, but another person can fling themselves across your path. And for all my dread of the unknown, I know if there is any chance that someday when I reread these thoughts (as I am wont to do) and I am sitting in a completely different room, in a different life from when I first wrote them, it will be because of other people, whom I found so wonderful and so interesting that I fell in step with them in spite of myself.

And all those other people will be because of my very first friend, the little boy who called me a nerd and didn't want to learn to read. Because, much to my surprise, and perhaps for the best, it is much harder to close your heart again than it is to open it the very first time. And if the first person you love is the right kind of person, then more will follow. We are, it turns out, all of us, built to love. And so, it would follow, we're built to live. And if you're like I am and you sometimes struggle to feel curious about yourself or your own life, that's when you need only look up, at whoever walks beside you. If you're short on reasons, it's as good a reason as any to stick around, if only to know what comes next, for the people you love. Not to mention for all the people you will love who you haven't even met yet, the books you haven't read yet, the books you've yet to finish, and even the stories that made you feel so much, you need to start them again.

It can be difficult, among even the best of friends, not to keep score, when you've changed each other's lives so absolutely, and imperceptibly. So perhaps, in some definitive way, I taught Caplan to read. But he taught me all of this, again and again each day, every time he turned the page.

So it was about life
and death and love
after all. Congratulations,
you genius douchebag.
XO, Hollis

P.S. if you try to take
this down and you fuck
up the wall, you're paying
our security deposit.

Acknowledgments

First, thank you to Sarah Barley, my editor, who is as brilliant as she is kind; your heart is in the book, and it is better for it. And to my agent, Elizabeth Bewley, who has guided me with tact and care from our very first phone call; your belief in this story, and in me, changed everything.

Thank you to every person at Sterling Lord, Flatiron Books, and Macmillan who sent me an email (or many)/ spent a minute (or a million) on this book: Flip Brophy, Szilvia Molnar, Amanda Price, Sydney Jeon, Megan Lynch, Emily Walters, Frances Sayers, Eva Diaz, Erin Kibby, Cat Kenney, Jen Edwards, Ally Demeter, Jennifer Edwards and the sales team, Keith Hayes, Jenna Stempel-Lobell, and Sara Robb with ScriptAcuity Studio, to name a few—and to Sarah Kelleher at Maria B. Campbell Associates. Thank you to David McCormick, who has been reading and encouraging my writing since I was in middle school. Thank you to Lorenzo Bergomi and Hannah Karzmer for their handwriting. And to Steve Amick, for his Michigan expertise and the secrets of the universe (Torch Lake).

Thank you to Anna, for keeping me sharp, and to Luke, for keeping me laughing. To Lisa and Brett, for your children, your guidance, your cheese sticks, and my first home in Brooklyn.

To Delia, Jake, Lennart, Carson, and Clara, for Tuesday nights—for making me write, and then making it better.

To Jeb, Harley, Lou, Emu, Grace, Hannah, Hannah, and Hannah, who make it easy to wake up every morning and believe in love, and who taught me to call more than one place home. There would be no book if you hadn't kept asking me what came next. Also to Josh, who is turning me into an optimist against all odds.

Thank you to all who hail from Montclair, to Glynnis and Sophie for the parts of high school worth remembering, and to Cristi, who got the whole porch to vote on the title and pick her favorite.

To Lily, who taught me to be too much, and to James, whom nobody taught to read.

To Annie, who had to be my neighbor, but didn't have to be my sister, and to her family, who followed suit.

Thank you always to Georgia, who had to be my sister but didn't have to be my best friend; to Walter, who loves better than any of us; and to my dad, whom he got it from.

Finally, Mom—I can't even begin, but you already know.

About the Author

Daisy Garrison graduated from Northwestern University and lives in Brooklyn with her friends. This is her first novel.